THE SUGAR CHRONICLES

OBSCURITY & INSANITY ON TOP OF A MOUNTAIN

JC THOMPSON

outskirts
press

CHAPTER 1:

THE LIFE OF A COLLEGE GRADUATE

I t was early autumn when I returned to the Carolina Mountains from my obscure and incoherent decadence abroad in a strange and foreign land known as Los Angeles, California. I had just completed my master's program in Journalism (which is a whole different story) and decided to move closer to home after my mother passed away from a brain hemorrhage and my father had been diagnosed with what some doctors referred to as Dementia and others called it Alzheimer's.

There was no reason to go completely home, or madly insane, mainly because I had nowhere to go. My mother had passed away when I was young and it had driven my father into depressed state of dementia and was placed in a nursing home for Alzheimer and dementia patients. Therefore, I returned to a resort area close to my hometown, just two hours away, deep in the Appalachian Mountains where I had lived during my tenure in college for my undergraduate degree in communications, where I majored in socializing, intoxication, obnoxiousness, female anatomy, and learned a few things about real life so that I could graduate. (That also is a completely different story: "The College Chronicles").

I had corresponded with a very small local weekly newspaper that hired me to cover special events and boring county government news, but when I arrived to start my job the owner of the newspaper had died and the spoiled children of said paper did not honor my promise of a job by the owner/editor of the small weekly paper. It had happened so suddenly in a span of a couple of weeks. I needed a job - and a drink; a double shot of Bacardi with a hint of Mountain Dew for flavor.

So, there I was, educated, jobless, and broke. I reunited with a former girlfriend whom I dated back in college, but suddenly I was emotionally unhinged from the ability to care for one woman that I had to spend more than a few hours with at a time listening to the inconsistencies of how I needed to make a commitment to fulfill her wishes as her own personal butler, baby step-daddy, paycheck and bitch-o-meter listener who should agree to staying at home in the evenings while she consistently went out with her friends, where I wasn't invited. There was no way that I was going to deal with anything that could make my life any worse than it already was. I had my car, my liquor, my cigarettes, and my health. All I needed was a job to pay some bills and visit my dad on my days off before the old fart completely forgot who I was and left me an orphaned young adult in a world full of self-pity, sex, alcohol and video games - which I had all of it, except the video games, because I had sold them for gas money.

I fancied myself an unemployed journalist. Therefore, living in a vacation / resort destination town in the Carolina Mountains, the high cost of living and limited journalism jobs forced me to look elsewhere in a maze of seasonal jobs which paid just enough to not get by on a wage considered unbelievable to all the rich who flooded this paradise of luxury vainness, foot powder odor and expensive closed-mindedness socialites who mingled very carefully amongst the poor, bearded, native-mountain population.

Recently single again, and broke, I noticed a job-posting on-line for a security guard at a resort on the very top of a mountain. The mountain, Sugar Peak, was where this high-rise condomini-um resort was located at the Peak - Un-creatively named "Sugar Peak", because, well, we already went over this not thirty sec-onds ago.

I called the number to find out more information:

"*Sugar Peak.*" a lady's voice said through the phone.

"Hi." It was all I could think of because I didn't know what my place was called or else I would return the favor and name the building from which I was calling.

"*Yes?*"

"So, this is Sugar Peak?" I said, suddenly realizing that so far all I had learned was that the number I dialed was the correct number.

"*Yes.*"

"I'm glad we got that out of the way, just in case I dialed a wrong number." I replied honestly as I looked for a place to put my ciga-rette out and finally finding a bourbon glass filled with last night's milk that I forgot to drink before I passed out on the sofa. A warm glass of milk helps me go to sleep but so does a bottle of whisky, rum or bourbon.

"*Yes.*" she said again.

Suddenly I had to think of a question just to get her to say 'no' or anything else.

"Is there somebody I can speak to about the job opening I saw for a security officer?"

"*Yes.*"

That didn't go as planned. I thought she would say for me to hold on a minute or name the person and or give me more information.

"And what would be the name of the person who I need to talk to about an interview, please?"

"That would be our General Manager, Donald." she said, happily.

"Now were getting somewhere!" I exclaimed quietly.

"What is your name, young man?"

"C.F. Abbott."

"I'm sorry?" she replied as if she knew who I was and was apologizing in a way to comfort me for knowing that I was who I was. Then I realized she didn't hear me clearly.

"C.F. Abbott." I said again.

"Sir, can you say that again I didn't hear you correctly."

"Do we have a bad connection?" I wondered aloud as I moved to the other side of the apartment.

"I'm sorry, you are mumbling a little." she said in an eerie happy tone.

"Charles Frazier Abbott. C.F. Abbott!" I mumbled loudly.

I did notice I was mumbling a little. I couldn't help it. My mumbling was existential, but more than likely my sub-conscious was inexplicably overcome with low self-esteem due to my recent self-inflicted bad decisions and lack of any sort of professional career after many years of higher learning and tens of thousands of dollars for an education that was supposed to get me a good-paying job in a career field that didn't exists in a crumbling economy at the end of the first decade of the 21st century. I was America's future; a poster-boy for the American dream of smoke-filled lungs, inebriation, and a chance to get a minimum wage job so that I could one day meet the girl of my dreams, have a family and work until I'm 92 years old. I just need to try not to mumble and everything would be fine.

"Hold on just a minute and let me transfer your call."

"Thank you."

"What?"

"Have a great day, lady!" I replied with a smile on my face as if she could see my forced gesture of politeness through my smoke-filled living room while I held my cell phone to my right ear, a drink in my left hand and the morning's breakfast on yesterday's orange shirt that I hadn't bothered to change due to my busy schedule of looking for job-postings online and in the once-a-week newspaper that I should have been working for as a reporter.

"Hello, this is Donald."

"Uh, yes..." my god, now I was saying 'yes'. "I was calling about the security officer job."

"What's your name?"

"C.F. Abbott."

"C what? Abbott?"

"C.F. - Charles F. Abbott"

"Do you have any experience in security work?"

"No, sir. I don't even have virus protection on my computer."

"Have you ever worked at a resort?"

"I've been snow skiing a few times and went to the beach once." I replied. I had been snow skiing and boarding a lot, and to the beach many times, but I was nervous and needed a job and it just kind of slipped out. I never meant to be a smart-ass; it just comes naturally.

"No experience? Never worked at a resort?"

"That's correct, sir." I reiterated as I began to feel the chance for the job slip between my fingers - no - that was my Bacardi and Mountain Dew mixed-drink as it fell to the floor and splashed across my bare feet as I heard the glass break.

I froze, hoping he didn't hear that and ask or wonder what just happened.

"Can you come in for an interview tomorrow at 9 am?"

"Yes!" I mumbled loudly and - happily, I think.

CHAPTER 2:

JOB SECURITY, SORT OF.

The next morning after over-indulging myself on basic cable television and cold pizza from two days ago, I stumbled across my kitchen in need of a cup of coffee. I soon remembered that the homeless shelter for stray penises, otherwise known as my ex-girlfriend, had taken the coffee maker with her when she moved in with some guy with a nice car and a lot of money. After looking at the time on the microwave I hurried to get dressed for my interview. As I rummaged through my clothing, which was few but looked like a plethora of clothing items when strewn across the floor, I wondered what to wear to a job interview as a security guard that paid a few cents above minimum wage. So I dressed as I would as a reporter and wore the only clean shirt I could find: a pink and blue knit collar shirt that my grandmother had given me for my birthday which looked vintage from 1987. I jumped into my khaki slacks and put on my best pair of tennis shoes and drove up Sugar Peak to the very top - to Sugar Peak Resort.

After the security officer at the gate grilled me about why I was there, he made a few phone calls and finally was told that I was supposed to be there for a job interview, I drove upwards a little longer until I arrived at the tall white building on the very top of the mountain.

At the front desk was a gentleman who looked to be about fifty years old. He looked like he had a mouth or lip problem as they seemed to crease together and pucker up like idiotic drunk girls do in their Facebook pictures.

As he began to speak it wasn't immediately evident that he seemed to be slightly slow or have some sort of learning disability, but as he explained to me in the longest way possible that his boss, Donald, would be with me in just a minute, it became clear that this guy wasn't the brightest crayon in the box.

"You can sit down in one of them comfortable chairs, Donald will be out here in just like about thirty seconds." he said, still making that strange lip-face, as he pointed at some expensive furniture in the lobby near the large rock fireplace.

"Okay, thank you." I replied as I oozed on over to a plush chair and had a seat near the fireplace.

I looked around at the large, beautiful lobby as I admired the large room. Suddenly I noticed a stain on my shirt. I looked up quickly wondering if anybody had noticed it as I nonchalantly tried to frantically wipe it off as if it was residue evidence. As the sweat beads began to mingle together at my hair line and make their journey down the slopes of my face I hurried to wipe away the stain with the palm of my hand like a cop was approaching me and this one was going to be the evidence to prove my guilt - whatever that might be - drinking too much Mountain Dew.

Once again, I looked up as my sunglasses fell off the top of my head. I watched as a man in a gray suit with a red tie walked in my direction. He didn't look like the police, although they were known to wear cheap suits that looked shiny from the light radiating into the lobby through the large windows that overlooked the smaller mountain ranges in the distance.

I quickly put my sunglasses in my left pocket as it bulged under protest due to the lack of vacant space from which my cigarettes and two lighters already had made their home in this pocket, long ago.

"Hi, I'm Donald Spacey, nice to meet you." he said as he extended his hand to shake mine.

"C.F. Abbott." I replied as I shook his hand.

"Let's go back to my office and talk a little, Mr. Abbott." he stated as he turned and motioned me towards the back, behind the concierge desk.

"Okay." I replied.

I followed him as we walked back behind the front desk and down a hallway which in reality wasn't very long, but at that moment either due to nervousness or something I might have accidentally taken instead of Tylenol made the hall stretch further as we continued to walk to his office which was at the end of the hall.

"My office is right here at the end of the hall." he said which alerted me to now I have a goal - to reach the end of the hall without passing out before I could sit down in one of two leather chairs positioned across the other side of his desk.

"Have a seat young man." he motioned for me to sit down, as he ever so professionally sat down as professional people do as they sit down at their desks in their nice chairs behind large mahogany desks.

"Do you like my new desk?" he asked proudly, as a way to start the conversation. "It's mahogany. It's very expensive compared to what most people expect."

I nodded as if I was listening to let him know that what he said matters in order to display good listening skills as was listed on my resume that was still on my kitchen counter because I had forgotten to bring it with me to the interview.

"I have no idea what that means, but I like the way the wood feels on my fingertips." I replied as I ran my right hand across the edge of his desk.

"Me too." he added.

I wasn't expecting him to say anything like that so I wasn't sure what to say back to him.

"Do you have a resume with you?" he asked.

"No," I replied, "I left it on my kitchen counter. I'm not forgetful nor am I irresponsible; I am just excited and nervous about my job interview. I need a job that pays money. You have to give me the job in order to get paid the money, so there's a lot of pressure on me right now."

"I see you handle pressure fairly well. You look calm, cool and collective."

"Thank you." I mumbled as I started by instinct or habit to reach for the cigarettes in my pocket.

"I was being sarcastic." he replied in a serious tone with a straight face.

Surprised by his remark I put a cigarette in my mouth and didn't realize what I had done.

He started laughing as if he had got me good with a joke. "I'm just joking with you!" he said as his face turned red with joyous laughter. "You should have seen the look on your face when I said that!" he laughed for a few more seconds until he began coughing and was distracted by a coughing spell that let me know that he, too, was a smoker.

I didn't know what to do so I looked around the room quickly at his framed degrees, awards and certifications, that hung on the walls in his office. I didn't want to be rude and look at them when he was talking, so I figured, while he was distracted by a cough that would want to make anyone take a nap afterwards, was the perfect time to get a glimpse of the man's achievements.

"That was funny." he added as his cough fit came to an end.

I kind of smiled and let out a few breaths of quiet fake laughter.

"So you don't have any experience in security." he asked again, as he did on the phone the day before.

"I lock my door to my apartment before I go to bed, and sometimes I leave the outside light on to deter people who are looking for a dark place to hang-out." I answered trying to boost my knowledge of 'security' to my potential future boss.

"Well, that's a good start!" he added.

"I like to keep a vigilant eye out for anything out of the... ordinary." I added.

He nodded as he listened. I continued.

"I'm a quick learner and a good listener. I do not have a problem with confrontation because as long as it leaves me alone, I leave it alone. I am college educated and would like to learn more about security so that I can do the best job I can while I am awake and sober." I explained to him as honestly as possible so that there would not be any secrets between us so that I could not later be fired for lying on my application.

He nodded, again, as he looked at me as if he was studying a piece of artwork that was interesting, yet didn't make sense but must have some sort of importance to be hanging on the wall in a famous museum as if it had a hidden meaning and it was his job to figure out exactly what that was.

"Okay, we'll give it a shot. I will hire you on a 90-day trial period." he said as he wrote something on a piece of paper.

"Thank you, Mr. Spacey, you will not regret it." I said knowing that I was probably lying on that part, but everything else was the truth.

He stood up and held out his hand so I did the same. As we shook hands I began to smile as if I was pleased to get a job as a security guard at the bottom of the barrel making a few dimes above minimum wage. It was the happiest most pathetic moment of my life - so far. At least I had a job and could now almost pay all my bills - which reminded me to pay my water bill so that I wouldn't have to bathe outside my apartment complex with the gardener's water hose again.

Welcome to our resort on top of the mountain!" he stated with a smile. "We will see you tomorrow! I'm sure you can find your way out?"

"There's only one way to find out!" I replied as we both laughed.

I walked out of his office and down the very short hallway.

"You have a good day now." the weird guy with the lip problem said to me as I walked by the front desk.

"I'll do my best." I replied as I looked at his mouth as it did that strange an unusual pucker-movement.

"My name is Freddie, by the way. What's yours?"

C. Lip Abbott - C.F. Abbott." I replied, quickly correcting myself as I continued on outside to my vehicle.

The sun shined dimly as I searched my pockets but I couldn't find my sunglasses. Tomorrow was going to be the first day of the rest of my employment on Sugar Peak. The sweet kiss of death couldn't come soon enough.

CHAPTER 3:

BITCH-SLAPPED IN THE FACE BY A SCARF

My eight-hour work-day didn't begin until three o'clock in the afternoon, so it left me plenty of time for self-indulgence in the form of sleeping late. The night before I had stayed up to watch a horror movie because I was too anxious to sleep, but I am not really much of a horror-movie kind of guy so then I definitely couldn't sleep after the movie. After restlessly rolling around and sitting up at every little spooky sound in the pitch blackness of my polluted room I eventually passed out right before sunrise thanks to self-medicating myself by taking several shots of rum as quickly as possible without passing the point of regurgitating in my toilet and slept until the sound of someone pounding on my front door. *Did I not pay the rent?* I wiggled my way out of my bed sheet and several blankets and slowly climbed out of bed. The knocking continued in sporadic rapid sounds like the spray of automatic gunfire in a bad neighborhood.

"Who is it?" I yelled through the door as I lit a cigarette and cautiously waited for a response.

"Open the door, you homo!" An aggressive voice yelled from the other side.

I was confused. I looked behind me as if maybe someone else was in my apartment and then came to the conclusion that this angry sounding man was at the wrong apartment door.

"There's no LGBT identifiable person in here! You have the wrong apartment!" I yelled through clinched lips that were holding my cigarette in place.

"Open the door, Abbott! I know that's you in there!" he replied.

I was shocked. The odds that two guys named Abbott living in the same apartment complex and one of them was gay and he found the wrong apartment was surprising, but not unheard of, probably.

"You got the wrong Abbott. Uh, I'm the straight one!" I explained as I looked at the clock on the stove and noticed I had 45 minutes to get ready and go to work.

"C.F. Abbott! I know who I'm looking for you asshole! It's me, Jake, now open the door!"

I quickly opened the door to see my old college roommate standing in front of me. He was a stocky guy with a Boy Scout personality who had never cared about anything unless it was related to guns, war, fighting, killing or explosions. He had his usual crew-cut military style haircut except now he actually was in the army - or marines - something like one of those.

"Jake!" I muttered through my cigarette, "What in the world, how did you end up here?"

"I was passing through town on my way back to report for duty in South Carolina. You told me where you were living a month ago so I thought I would surprise you! How have you been you lazy piece of shit!? It's so good to see you, buddy!" he said as he grabbed me forcefully around the neck and slapped the shit out of my back as I could feel last night's rum and fried bologna sandwich awake from its slumber in my stomach and resisting being pushed upwards by these forceful yet friendly slaps across my upper back.

"Well, don't just stand there like an idiot, are you going to invite me in?" he asked as he stepped inside my apartment. He looked around and didn't even mention or notice the mess as it probably looked and felt like 'home' back when we were roommates in college.

"Goddamn, I miss this place!" he said with a hint of nostalgia as a smile came to his face as he looked across the kitchen, into the living room.

"We never lived here, Jake. I just moved here not long ago." I replied as I thought he just missed the good times back in college.

"No? It feels like we did. I miss it. It's good to be back!" he added as he gave me another friendly hard slap on the back one more time.

"How long are you going to be here, in town?" I asked, knowing I had to get to work soon and didn't know if he was here to stay a day or two.

"Actually," he replied looking at his military watch, "I didn't have time to stop, it wasn't in my schedule, but I couldn't drive through without seeing my good buddy! It just wouldn't be right."

I could tell he was excited to see me but also was in a hurry to go shoot guns and kill something with a grenade or rocket launcher.

"Oh," I replied, "I'm glad I got to see you. Sorry it couldn't be longer."

"That's what I came here to tell you," he said as we walked back to the front door. "I'm getting married! Yessir. I'm getting married. Can you believe that?"

"No." I answered.

"It's true, buddy! She's a hot piece of ass too! You know the military supports marriage."

"That's good." I replied.

"Yeah, the government encourages service members to get married. It's more money, guaranteed ass when you get home from deployment and you get paid more!

"That's great." I said still in shock that he was getting married.

"Yeah it is great! She's great! I can't wait." he added.

"Congratulations." I said as I gave him a hard slap on his back.

"Thanks Abbott. I appreciate it." he said as he stepped outside of my apartment and started walking away.

"Okay, be careful driving back to your fort-base place..." I said as he walked away.

"Don't worry about me!" he replied. "If some fucker on the highway gets in my way, I'll just run over them with my truck!"

"Okay, you do that - sounds good." I said not ever knowing how to respond to Jake's comments half the time. "Be safe!" I waived but he wasn't looking. I went back inside and closed the door.

"That was random." I thought to myself as I lit another cigarette and took off my pajamas and walked into the bathroom to get in the shower.

⸺⸺●⸺⸺

I drove up to the main gate as the same young, over-weight, bald security guard with a discombobulating look greeted me with his usual question.

"Can I help you?" he asked as he wiped remnants of potato chips away from his mouth.

"Today's my first day," I replied through my open driver's side car window. "I'm working security here, too."

"One minute." he replied as he walked back into the guard/ gatehouse and picked up a telephone. In a few moments he walked back outside to my vehicle.

"You would think that they would have told me you were coming." he said as he gave me a temporary parking pass that was meant to hang from my rearview mirror. I forced a slight smile as he handed it to me and I threw it on the dash of my car.

"You need to hang that up on the rearview mirror, please." he told me as he stood there waiting for me to do so.

I didn't say anything as I just waited for him to open the gate and let me into the resort.

After a few long seconds I looked at him to see him still standing next to my car waiting me to hang up my parking pass on my rearview mirror.

"I don't wanna be late on my first day, it makes a bad impression." I said, hinting for him to open the gate.

I grabbed the damn thing and hung it where it was supposed to be (on the rearview mirror) as I uncomfortably smiled again and waited for the gate to open.

As I drove on around the curvy road up to the gigantic obstruction on the top of the mountain, I came to another gate which did not have an attendant. I figured they could see me on camera as I waited for the second gate to open.

Nothing happened.

I lit a cigarette as I sat in my vehicle wondering if I was at the wrong gate or somehow nobody noticed my presence.

"Can I help you?" said an irritated voice of a woman from a speaker at the gate. I was tempted to place a fast food order for shits and giggles but that would not be a great way to start the first day at my new job that I ever-so-grudgingly accepted. It was better than being homeless and starving to death.

"I'm C.F. Abbott," I answered, "I just started working here, today."

I could hear a sigh through the intercom and then the gate opened. I began to realize that I was going to need to leave for work ten minutes earlier than planned if I had to go through this rig-a-ma-roo of "one gate - two gate, please open the gate."

I continued to drive around the tall resort building and found the employee lot. It was easy to spot because it was the only group of cars that looked as if they had had a hard-long life. Dents, dings, rust and smelly brakes filled the employee parking lot with a sense that these cars didn't belong in the sea of brilliant shiny sparkling paint on snooty high-nosed classy vehicles who seemed to separate themselves from the average vehicles parked off to the side. It reminded me of a high school lunch room where the poor and weird kids had to sit off to one corner while the social elite pretty girls and athletes dominated the center of the lunch room. Now I knew what it felt like to sit in the corner of the lunch room and suddenly felt ashamed of not only having been one of those cars in the center of the lunch room but of also parking my old faded blue hotrod in the corner with the other worn-out vehicles.

I parked in the next available spot in the employee parking and proceeded to walk in the employee entrance to the resort.

The hallway entrance was gray and had a dungeon-like feel to it as I walked past the loud water pipe pump area and down a long wide depressing hallway. I nodded and waved or smiled to house-keepers, maintenance workers, and whomever else I passed on my way to the main lobby.

At the front desk was Freddie. His lip problem was the first thing I noticed, again, as his mouth slowly continued to move in and out of a fish-like shape.

"Howdy there!" he said as his beady eyes locked on to mine.

"Hey." I replied uncomfortably as I had no idea of where I was supposed to go or what I was supposed to be doing.

"How are you today?" he asked.

"Good." I mumbled.

"Can I help you?" he asked.

I was beginning to wonder if that was the standard line for everyone to say, but as it annoyed me slightly in my sense of being half excited about starting my job and half due to my hangover, I nonetheless replied, "Today is my first day of work and I'm not really sure who I am supposed to talk to or where to go."

He looked at me as if he was disappointed at my lack of information as to where I was supposed to go.

I stood there a moment and moved my eyes around as if I was in trouble for something that I had no clue about what I did or didn't do.

"I'm working security." I finally said, hoping that would give this odd gentleman behind the front desk a clue as to whom I needed to speak with, in order to properly report to work.

"Let me find somebody." he replied as he picked up a hand-held walkie-talkie radio and spoke. "Front desk to security."

"*This is security, go ahead front desk.*" replied a voice over the radio.

"I have a young man who said he's working for security. Today's his first day and wants to know what he's supposed to be doing." Freddie said.

I obviously did not know anything about my job yet, but I figured that other employees would seem to know a little about each department and could have helped me a little more than him not knowing the slightest clue of where I should go or which person I should report to for my job.

"Hey!" said a loud voice, taking me completely by surprise. It was Donald Spacey, the General Manager of the resort.

"Hello!" I replied.

"How's your first day going, so far?" he asked enthusiastically.

"Good!" I replied, not knowing what to say, although that wasn't necessarily the truth.

"Are you ready to keep this place secure?" he asked with a smile.

"Absolutely," I nodded, "I will do my best to make sure this place is... secure and - stuff."

"Good, good!" he smiled as he walked away. "Welcome aboard! Glad to have you as our newest employee!"

"Someone should be with you shortly to help you get started." Freddie said as I thanked him and we returned to standing around in awkward silence.

Out from the service entrance I could see a small man in the usual gray and black security uniform. He was little and had big teeth with a grin of that of a creepy toy maker from 18th century Europe. As he walked closer I noticed he had a twitch in his left eye and spoke with a slight stammer which I shall leave out in the dialogue of this story, as not to seem to be making fun of his unfortunate habit.

"Hello," he said as he greeted me with a handshake, "my name is Security Steve, you must be Security Charles Frazier Abbott."

"C.F. Abbott, I replied, correcting him, "C.F. will be just fine."

"Security C.F.!" he replied with excitement.

"C.F." I added again, not wanting my new 'first name' to be 'Security'. "C - F."

"Security C.F.!" he exclaimed again with a big-toothed smile and a quick clap of his hands.

"Okay." I said realizing that as weird as it sounded, I didn't have a choice and would now be called 'Security C.F.'.

"Welcome, Security C.F, to the top of the mountain!" Freddie blurted with his arms stretched out wide and a smirk on his face from behind the front desk.

"Thanks, a lot, Front-Desk-Freddie." I replied not wanting to sound like a smart ass, yet not sure how to reply. It made sense.

"Front desk -" Security Steve snickered, "Freddie."

"Hey, that's not funny not one bit." Freddie said with a pout as he picked up a pen and pretended to write something but it looked more like he was drawing circles. "I've got work to do, so y'all need to go somewhere else."

"Let me go ahead and give you a tour of the resort." Security Steve said.

"Good stuff." I replied.

"Hey there!" Donald Spacey said with a smile, as he stepped between me and Security Steve, "First things, first! You need to go see the office manager and fill out your Federal and state tax forms before you get started! We have to keep all that on file from the day you start."

"Okay," I replied non-enthusiastically, "Where is that? Who do I see?"

"That would be Amelia Gant, the Office Manager. She's down the hall and on the left." he said with a friendly smile.

He was a little weird, but nice. He seemed like a good guy.

"Alright, thanks." I said as I slowly walked towards Amelia Gant's office.

There, sat a lady who looked very unhappy with both life and work. She rolled her eyes and sighed as she hit the 'delete' button on her computer's keyboard to re-type whatever it was that she had messed up.

"Hi," I said, "I'm C.F. Abbott, the new security officer. I was told to come see you to fill out my tax forms."

She smiled a big fake smile, "Just a moment, let me get those for you."

'Thank you." I replied.

"Uh-huh," she said as she opened her desk drawers and searched for the tax forms. "So are you from here, you look familiar."

"No, not technically," I replied, "I went to college here a few years ago, but I just moved back not long ago."

"Oh, dropped out?" she said, as she handed me the forms, "don't worry, I dropped out too. I hated school, but loved the parties."

"Uh, no, actually," I felt awkward, but wasn't going to lie, "I graduated with a B.A., and then went on to journalism school in California.

I think it insulted her a little, but I didn't mean to cause any harm to her ego. "Fill these out. Bring them back tomorrow.' she said as she handed me the appropriate tax forms and went back to typing on her computer.

"Thank you." I said, before leaving.

She just raised an eyebrow and kept on working.

I found my way back to the lobby to follow Security Steve on my tour of the resort.

We walked and talked - Well, I mainly listened while Security Steve, my department boss, stammered and stuttered his way through a tour of the resort. He was a really nice guy, just slightly weird, with a speech impediment.

We went through the halls of every floor of the resort. To the banquet rooms, other lobbies, recreational areas, pools, spas, locker and laundry rooms and on to the employee office and break room areas.

"This is the break room." he said, just in case I didn't notice by the obvious signs of a large table with chairs, a kitchen, microwave and all the other stuff and appliances that make a break room a break room and a kitchen a kitchen, which was good for him to explain because by that point of my grand tour I actually wasn't paying attention as I should have been, but lost in the thought that this was now my clear and present future, since my present future wasn't very clear when I was at home or out with friends drinking a few too many or whatever I may be doing during my personal time of self-pity and deprecation.

From around the corner from the depths of the back of the main building where the maintenance workers had their own little place of operation where sounds of squealing saws and strange hissing noises from water pipes drifted towards the employees' break room came a scary individual of frightening proportions walking towards me. He was built like a burned-out retired pro-wrestler. His gray hair went in all different directions as if he was a long-lost descendant, perhaps through a bastard-child lineage of Albert Einstein. He had a stern look on his face and as he walked ever so sturdily closer, I noticed that he had one eye that was dead. It wasn't very noticeable, but I notice the unimportant and never pay attention to the obvious - well, somewhat, sometimes.

"Hey, is this the new guy?" the man said as he poured himself a cup of coffee.

"Yes," replied Steve, this is C.F. Abbott, the new security officer."

"Hey man, nice to meet you." I replied as if an angry outlaw biker had me backed in the corner and there was no way out. He seemed very scary, but I smiled and waited for a friendly response.

"Welcome to Sugar Peak. I'm Jerry!" he said with a friendly teddy bear smile as he walked over and shook my hand. "If you got any questions when I'm around feel free to ask me and I'll help you if I can."

"Thanks Jerry," I replied, "I'll keep that in mind."

"Hey, no problem because there's some people here who will be willing to help you and then there's others who will try to get you in trouble for something they did because you're new and don't know no better." he said as he sipped on his coffee and walked away.

"I appreciate it." I added, as he continued to walk away without any slight indication that he heard me.

"Well, that - that - concludes, it concludes our tour." Steve said as I started to notice his stumbling, stuttering sentences more carefully - which remember, I will not write his stammering, stuttering voice in here unless it can't be avoided in the story for effect or persuasion. "You can start working now on the things that I told you about." he continued. "Just look over the check-list and do what is on there and write down your times and initial by each thing that you do on the check-list."

"Alright." I nodded. "I guess I'll start by walking each floor, if that is okay?" not really sure if it mattered, because it seemed this place, at least the security department, was more disorganized than myself would be on a Sunday morning with a hangover trying to figure out how to shit, shower, and shave when I couldn't even find my bedroom the night before in a fit of drunken discombobulating vomiting.

As I walked each and every floor of the high-rise resort, I noticed many condos with their door wide open. I found this very shocking because not one person in their right mind would do such a thing in Los Angeles. Televisions were blaring for the unfortunate souls whom could not hear as well as others. A mixture of sounds from left-wing and right-wing political shows, daytime trash talk shows, and soaps mixed in the hallways into a discontent of noise with a sour taste.

"Hey, partner! Hey you!" was the sound of a loud south-western accent as I turned around to see if the man was talking to me.

There stood an older gentleman wearing a leather jacket and a red scarf with a WWII fighter pilot cap and swimming goggles.

"Me?" I asked quietly in disbelief as I pointed to myself.

"Yeah, you!" he replied in a loud-sounding voice. "You mind giving me a hand for a minute, partner? It won't take but I minute. Come on and help an old man with something? "He motioned for me to come in his condo as he walked on inside with a slight limp.

I, cautiously from a slight distance, followed him inside and was automatically amazed at the decorative style of his adobe-themed home. There were pictures of military planes and fighter pilot groups hung on the living room walls. The colors of the walls and trim were pastel and the furniture matched his south-western accent.

In the living room was a photographer and a burgundy chair with a large fan sitting several feet away out of view.

"I'm having my picture taken for a newspaper article and I need your help." the gentleman said.

"Magazine. It's for a magazine." the photographer corrected him.

"Oh, who the hells cares! Magazine, newspaper, whatever! It doesn't matter." the gentleman replied. "All that matters is that we get these pictures taken, but there's a problem. The goddamned fan quit working so now my scarf won't flutter backwards like I'm in one of those old open cockpits."

"Okay." I hesitated, wondering what I was supposed to do to help. "What do you need me for?"

"I want you to stand behind me and hold the ends of the damn scarf and shake 'em around like it's blowing in the wind! Can you do that for me, partner?"

"Uh... alright." I said. "Why not, this isn't the weirdest thing I've ever been asked to do, so... sure."

"Great! Let's get started." he exclaimed as he sat down in the chair and posed more as if he was having his picture taken in a chair than in a cockpit of a plane. "What are you waiting for, partner? Grab the damn ends of the scarf and start shaking."

I grabbed the ends of his scarf and stepped back out of view of the camera and started flapping the scarf that was around his neck as if it was in the breeze.

"Take the damn pictures!" he exclaimed with a big cheese grin on his face.

The photographer began snapping off a few shots as the flash blinded us both.

"Any of these pictures got me with my damn eyes open? Jesus. That flash is brighter than a pale fat ass in a string bikini. I can't see shit!" he replied.

I kept shaking the scarf.

"Yes, they're great. Just keep smiling because we're almost finished" the photographer replied as he kept taking pictures.

"What's your name, partner?" the gentleman said, speaking to me.

"Abbott. C.F. Abbott." I replied.

"C.F. Abbott?" he asked

"Yessir."

"You got a real first name, or just some initials?" he asked.

"I just go by 'Abbott'." It's been that way since middle school.

"Well, where the hell you go to anyways, a military school?"

he asked as he kept turning his head for a second and then looking back at the camera quickly and smiling.

"No, my coach called me Abbott and then so did everyone else." I explained.

"Why in the hell didn't they call you C.F.?" he asked.

I shrugged. "C.F. isn't my real initials, there was a typo at the DMV because I made that up when I registered for college as a joke and then it actually stuck by some weird computer error, so I gave myself names for those initials – Charles Frazier."

"No shit?"

"True story." I added. (Read the prequel to find out why.)

"Well, I'll be a sumbitch." he laughed. "My name is Scotty. You can call me Scotty. I'm a retired Navy pilot and now I live here with my wife." he said as we shook hands.

"Look at me, and stop shaking hands." the photographer squawked.

"Ah, you shut the hell up. I think were done here." Scotty said as he grabbed the scarf and pulled it off his neck and tossed it towards the photographer.

"Thanks for your help Abbott!" he said as he shook my hand again and slid a five dollar bill in the palm of my right hand.

"Thank you, sir." I replied.

"What the hell did I tell you? My name is Scotty! Call me Scotty!"

"Okay, Scotty. Thank you."

"No, thank you, partner!" he said.

I walked out of the condo and back into the hallway and continued my security walk down the hall.

"That's beer money!" Scotty yelled from his doorway. "Don't spend one damn dime on anything but a beer! You deserve it and beer money deserves to be spent only on beer, damn it!"

"Okay, will do!" I replied as I turned to wave and kept walking.

Beer money, well, wasn't that nice. Too bad I'm not patient enough to drink beer. I like to get to the point and liquor helps me get to the buzz via the short-cut. I still had a few spirits left to drink at my apartment and needed gas more than anything else. So, I put that tip in my gas tank on my way home from my first day at work on the Peak of Sugar Mountain.

CHAPTER 4:

LET ME INTRODUCE YOU TO MY NEIGHBOR

There was one apartment I had to walk past to get to my own. I avoided the guy who resided in said apartment with a passion, because he was weird and creepy. Although most times it was quite easy to sneak on past the door quietly, the days that he sat outside I dreaded with a passion as if the bubonic plague was waiting for me and there was nothing I could do but accept my inevitable fate of it following me back to my own door and annoying the shit out of my ears. He looked like a tweaker who acted like a meth addict who substituted his addiction with cocaine or some other form of hyper-active narcotic which caused uncontrollable rambling with injective annoyance. Whenever he caught a glimpse of me he would talk about his day or his thoughts on the world and follow me to my door which I would politely close in his face. This would be followed by a sometimes stern, yet other times light, knock on my door as he would continue talking.

"I have to take a shit! I can't talk right now! Sorry!" would be my excuse that I would yell through the other side of the door as I plopped down on the sofa and turned up the television to drown out his babblings until he went away, only to bother me on another occasion.

I woke up in a few hours after somehow drifting off into a quick and deep sleep. The TV seemed very loud in my head as I awoke. I searched for the remote to lower the volume, but it had disappeared in my sleep. I ran my hands through the couch cushions as I discovered something with my fingers that felt like gloss paper. I pulled it out to see a picture of me and my ex-girlfriend that had been taken during a party back in college. This was, at one time, her couch, sofa, piece of furniture - whatever you wish to call it - but I had no idea why it was in-between the cushions or who put it there. I gazed at it for a moment as I looked past her to see some of my old friends in the background: Kaelo Mack, Ducky and Carp, who were all making faces. (Read the prequel).

Suddenly the loneliness and depravity of my situation poured upon me as I felt like a complete loser and began to feel sorry for myself. At no time in my life did I ever feel that I would be alone, broke, unhappy and unsure of how much lower my life could sink. I felt as if I had been abandoned by the universe and was now paying the price for my wild extravagance fun of my youth. Where did I go wrong with my plans in life? Heck, there could be a hundred different times that caused me to be where I am today, but it didn't matter - here I was - living a life I had never wanted. The only thing I knew was that I had to keep looking for a better job, particularly one in journalism or some form of writing and get the hell out of this dump and away from the pathetic excuse for a job as a security guard. Don't misunderstand me - I didn't think I was too good for my job as a security guard, but rather I felt that if this was all that there was then I had obviously wasted many years and lots of money trying to educate myself to have a better life than minimum wage. The job didn't make me feel like a complete failure as much as I made myself feel like a complete loser. Only one day behind me at work and I already hated my job as much as I now hated my life.

I heard a knock at the door and then the faint sound of the crazy guy's voice saying "It's not so much that rainbows are where the color of birds comes from, as much it is that God only lets of have those colors because we don't deserve any more colors than that! He won't give us more because we don't deserve them. We couldn't possibly be able to comprehend other colors although green birds don't seem as common as yellow. And where's black? I say make them pink. That'll show people how life really is because you never see pink in the rainbow!"

"Shut the fuck up I'm trying to sleep!" I yelled.

"Sorry..." he said through the other side of the door.

I eventually felt bad, but at the moment all I wanted was to go back to sleep after a shot of rum and a nice hot shower. I need-ed a girlfriend, but who in their right mind would date me when I couldn't even afford to take myself out to dinner? Time for a drink, while in the shower, so I could go to bed sooner.

CHAPTER 5:

THE DEVIL IS MY CO-WORKER

Hilary was a mean fat alcoholic bitch who looked like a clown and hated anyone who smiled, anyone whom was liked by many people and/or did their job correctly and was complimented by resort guests, condo owners and other employees. She hated everyone that did their jobs correctly.

When someone needed a maintenance employee, a bell hop, security officer or whomever her favorite line was "Well, I'll see what I can do, but there's no guarantee. It seems like I'm the only one who does any work around here!" As if nobody else gave a damn. I'm not saying that I put my whole heart and soul into my job, but I did what I was told to do and did it correctly just for shear fact that I didn't want to get fired, because it was a recession and I need my paycheck, no matter how pathetic it was and no matter how much I dreaded my job - it paid the bills. Sort of.

Hilary not only tried to make herself look irreplaceable by falsely insulting everyone else, but in the process, she gave guests and homeowners at the resort a bad image of all other employees unless they knew first-hand that someone was reliable and only then would they realize that her contempt and jealously of everyone else was misleading. Although it wasn't right, it did keep everyone on their toes because they had to prove to everyone that Hilary was full of shit, and work harder to prove to everyone that each employee (most of them) were dependable, reliable, hard-working and most of all, didn't like that mean-ass fat clown bitch and one day would get what was coming to her.... A premature heart attack at a young age from being overweight and drinking herself right into the hospital - but that wouldn't happen for a while, and since nobody knew that was going to happen, yet, we all had to put up with her and only wish that one day our boss, Donald Spacey, would wise up and fire her fat drunk ass before we all jumped her in the parking lot and took her down like a dozen cave-men with sticks hunting a mighty elephant in the dangerous plains of ancient Africa. The difference is: Ancient man hunted the elephants for food to feed the tribe for most of the winter, and although cannibals could probably survive off Hilary's meat for a long time, most employees and myself, just wanted her to go away and stop annoying, aggravating and sticking her pudgy nose in our business. She was the antagonist - in a slight unimportant way, the villain in a superhero story, the evil witch created in a drug-influenced novel, the bully in the classroom and the bad smell of a fart or diarrhea from someone's asshole.

"Two young couples checking in for the weekend need help unloading their car." Hilary said to me with a smirk of hate on her face. "The two girls in the group think you're cute. They said something about it when you walked by a few minutes ago. I told them that if they want you to help their boyfriends to unload their car to, first of all, stick to the men they already have, because you don't make nearly enough money to drive a car as nice as theirs, and second, to wash their luggage after you touch it because I wouldn't trust you not to have something dirty!"

"Why would you say something like that?" I asked, confused

and in shock.

"I mean, I don't even know you, but I know a pathetic lazy dumb-ass when I see one," she said with a smile and a laugh, "and you have that written all over your face!"

After a second of standing there, dumb-founded, I rolled my eyes and brushed it off as I went outside to help the two girls and two guys unload their BMW. In the tall shrubbery against the building I heard a rustling noise and I heard the sound of a pump-action water gun, at least that's what it sounded like. Suddenly a tall slender older man in a maintenance uniform stepped out of the tall shrubbery with a device strapped on his back that looked like a flamethrower used in the jungles of the pacific islands during World War Two.

"Hey there, young fella!" said the maintenance worker with an awkward smile. "Hope I didn't startle you a little bit! I'm just spraying these here bushes, trying to get rid of the weeds and all that other junk that ain't supposed to be in there. So, you're the new guy? Welcome to Sugar Mountain! I think you might like it here. That's up to you though. Some do, some don't. It just depends on what you make it and whether or not this is a place you plan on being a long time or just until you find something different - 'cause you know - lots of people come through here wantin' a job, but they don't stay long."

I nodded, knowing that I was only working here until I could finally get a job in journalism - or something better than this. "Yeah, maybe that's me, too. I don't know... I'm just glad to be employed." I replied.

"My name's Rocky. What's yours?" he said.

"Like the boxer?" I asked, never having actually met anyone in real life named 'Rocky'.

"Do I look like a damn boxer to you?" he asked annoyingly, as if he had heard that a lot.

"Sorry." I replied. "I'm - well, just call me Abbott."

"Nice to meet you, Abbott!" he replied. As he threw up his fists in sort of a boxing position. "Watch out now!" he said pretending to throw a few punches.

"Whoa, look out!" I replied. Suddenly I felt a soft hand on my left shoulder as it moved across my back. It was one of the girls in the couples' group that I was supposed to help unload their luggage.

"We've already got everything taken care of." she replied. "Our boyfriend's muscles are apparently bigger than we realized."

"Okay, good. Hey, just let me know if I can help with anything else." I replied, feeling bad that I didn't help guests as I was supposed to do. I was distracted by the weird maintenance man in the tall shrubbery, but I guess it was okay because the girls weren't mad, and apparently once the boyfriends saw me they decided to do it themselves, and besides, all this is new to me. I had a lot to learn, more to see and everything at this crappy job to get used to and learn my way around. In a way I got lucky on that one because they had lots of heavy-looking luggage and I was sure to have struggled with not wanting to drop or break anything that wasn't mine. If I was meant to be a bell-hop then I wouldn't be wearing a security uniform.

I walked back inside and had no choice but to walk by the front desk.

"Guess they didn't want to have to sanitize their bags." Hilary said with a snicker.

It was only my second day, but sometimes you have to let someone know where they stand and set the ground rules of social acceptability in order to let someone know that you won't put up with certain behavior. I stopped. I turned around and simply replied, "Well, they asked if you could help them but then I helped them realize that you wouldn't be able to bring the bags inside the condo because the doors aren't wide enough!"

"Gasp!" is what she said - it wasn't the word itself, of course, but the sound itself and for once the rest of the day, and the whole rest of the week she didn't say one more thing to me, unless there was no other choice.

After work that day the time clock ate my timecard. It was eleven o'clock at night and nobody on the 'night crew' could help me. So I just left it sitting on the table that was sitting below the time card machine, hoping that someone in the morning would notice it and fix it for me. I didn't know who to call or tell since I didn't really receive an 'information packet' or was informed on who to talk to if the time clock ever ate my timecard. Knowing my luck, I was probably the first.

The older maintenance worker that I had met early that day in the bushes was leaving as I was. His old red pick-up truck was parked next to my crappy blue hot rod.

"So, I hear you came here all the way from California." Rocky said, "What brought you here?"

"Yeah," I replied as I unlocked my car. "I went to school out there, but that's over and I moved back this way and I needed a job."

"The economy is tough, boy. I'll give you that so I can understand you working here, even with your fancy college degree." he replied. "I wish you the best of luck with everything."

"Thank you." I replied, appreciating hearing something sincere for once.

CHAPTER 6:

BEER BOTTLES, BONE HEADS & BITTER WOMEN

pulled up to the first gate at the gatehouse and the same security guard opened the window and politely said, "Can I help you?"

I'm sure that he sees a lot of people, but the idea that he might have either remembered my crappy blue car or my face was a possibility that didn't happen.

"I work here." I replied through a clinched cigarette as I pulled off my sunglasses and smiled, hoping my face looked slightly familiar.

"What's your name?" he asked.

"Abbott," I replied, "C.F. Abbott."

"Oh, okay." he said, as I hoped he now remembered. "Let me call the front office."

"Seriously?"

"Yeah," he replied, "It won't take but just a minute, sir."

"I really don't want to be late, again." I added, but he didn't hear me.

Another car pulled up to the gate beside me and suddenly my gate arm went up. Assuming, obviously, that he opened my gate to let me through I proceeded to pull forward - just in time for the gate to fall on the roof on my car. It made a horrible sound as if someone had just fallen on my vehicle. I screeched to a stop after only moving a few feet.

With a broken cigarette in my mouth, my sunglasses on crooked and my black security ball cap was sideways on my head, all from hitting my head on the door of my car as I got out of my car to see what the hell happened. I noticed the security guard standing there with his hands on his head and a look of a horrific "I'm sorry" across his face.

"What the hell?" I mumbled through my clinched cigarette. "Why did you do that?" I was dumbfounded.

"I am so very sorry!" he yelled as he hurried over to my car to survey the damage. "Did it hurt your car?"

"I gotta be honest," I replied, astonished, yet not upset, "I don't exactly drive the newest nicest vehicle, so it's really hard to say."

"So... did it mess it up?" he asked again as he nodded as if he agreed with me, but didn't understand what I was saying.

"No."

"Are you sure?" he asked again, looking at my crappy blue car as if all the dents, dings and rust could have possibly just accrued due to the gate arm dropping across the roof of my car.

I knew this would be a losing conversation so I just answered. "Yes."

"Oh, no!" he replied, "I am so very sorry!"

"What happened?" I asked, still confused at the whole situation. "Why did the gate fall on my - my, perfectly nice, brand new, dent-free car.... That I love so much?" That was obviously sarcasm.

"Like I said, I am so very sorry! It was an accident."

"No kidding?"

"I was opening the gate arm for the other car but I accidentally opened your gate and then I realized what I had done and tried to close it to prevent a security breach."

"A what?" I asked.

"A security breach!" he replied. "You didn't have clearance yet to go up to the top."

"But I work here!" I yelled.

He just stood there more confused than I was.

"You do?"

"Yes!" I exclaimed. "Now look at my car. It's all - beat up and looks like it's old and - crappy." I wasn't blaming him, obviously, but I definitely felt like verbally milking the situation and making him feel bad since he obviously wasn't qualified to raise and lower a gate arm.

"Please don't try to get me fired for this. I am so sorry. It was an accident." he pleaded.

Suddenly I felt bad for him. He probably needs his job as bad, if not more, than I need mine.

"I'm not going to try and have you fired." I replied, "Just remember this car and my face next time. I'm late for work every day so far this week because I have to go through this gate and then another gate up top, and by the time I clock in for work it's like seven or eight minutes after three o'clock. I need this job just like everybody else."

"No problem! Absolutely!" he said.

"Just remember my car from now on." I said again as I got in my car.

"Trust me, I won't never forget it now." he added.

"Hey," I said before driving away, "Why were you going to open the gate for the other car, but not mine?"

"Because it has an employee sticker in the bottom right-side of the windshield." he answered as if that was common knowledge.

"Why Don't I have one?" I asked.

"I don't know," he shrugged, "did you ask for one?"

"No! I didn't know there was such a thing."

"Oh," he replied, "ask the front office. They'll give you one."

"Okay, thanks. I'll do that." I said.

"My name is Bo. What's yours?" he asked.

"Abbott." I replied. "I work security in the building."

"Nice to meet you, Bo."

"You too, uh..."

"You forgot my name already, didn't you?" I asked.

"Yeah. Sorry." he replied.

"Abbott. C.F. Abbott."

"Nice to meet you, C.F. Abbott."

"You, too, Bo."

"Have a good day!" he yelled as I drove on up the hill.

I waved out of the side window.

When I walked in the service entrance and into the time-clock room I noticed I had a new timecard with my previous hours added to the new card. Somebody took care of it. I was glad that the whole day, so far, wasn't summed up by a gate dropping on my car. Thank God I was too poor to drive something nice or else then I probably would have been pissed about the whole thing, but then again, if I did drive a nice car because I wasn't poor then I wouldn't be working in this paradise of a hell-hole anyways.

"Hey, partner!" said a familiar voice.

"Hey, Scotty!" I replied. "How's everything?"

"Great! Well, I got this damn leg that's been giving me problems so I'm using this cane just to be on the safe side, but it's not too bad." he said as I walked with him towards the main lobby. "I'm taking the wife on an old-fashioned picnic today and then we're going on a paddleboat ride in one of those goddamn paddleboats. They are so slow and boring, but that's what the wife wants to do, so be it."

"That sounds nice." I said.

"Well, it's our anniversary. So later on tonight we'll go out to dinner and do the whole dance."

"Congratulations!" I added, "How many years now?"

"Fifty-eight years!" he replied as if he was astonished, yet with a smile. "We got married at twenty-two and never looked back, but I have to be honest with you Abbott, if I knew I was going to live this long I might have waited a few more years before ending my life as I knew it!"

"That's funny. Well, you two have fun!" I replied.

"Will do, Abbott! Thank you."

It was nice to see two old people in love and still going on dates. I'm glad I didn't have to deal with that, yet. Yet.

Chad was coming on shift when I arrived. I had known him from when I lived in the area back in my under-grad college days. He had been a bouncer at a few of the local bars and clubs near-by and worked at the fitness center where my friends and I had worked-out (somewhat) when we were younger, dumber and - in college. Several years ago, after a tragic accident, he had pulled his life to-gether and taken responsibility for his bad choices. So the next bad choice he made was to get a job at Sugar Peak as a Front Desk re-ceptionist. He was a good person with a whacky sense of humor and later would become a good friend of mine. I've lost touch with him since our days as employees at Sugar Peak, so I guess he was a good friend, I just need to do a better job at staying in touch with people, but you know, sometimes when you make friends as easily as I do it's difficult to stay in touch with everybody. You just have to roll the dice of life and let it ride and see what happens, who shows up in your life and who doesn't, and every now and then, on a quiet rainy day, make a few phone calls to long lost friends, if there not dead.

"Long time, no see, Abbott!" Chad said with a big grin on his face. I could tell that his days of indulging in steroids and other un-natural substances were behind him as he still looked slightly de-formed with big muscles, yet smaller in size than he once had been. His hair had begun to fall out and his head looked ungodly larger than I remembered. He was very friendly now, unlike his raging bad-temper days of the past and always seemed to have something nice to say to people, unless they deserved otherwise.

"Hey Chad, how have you been, man." I replied, happy to see him too.

"Great!" he replied enthusiastically, as he asked me simply to the point. "What in the hell are you doing here?"

"I work here." I replied, not knowing if the security uniform wasn't enough to explain my presence or if he meant 'here' in the region.

"I know that!' he replied with a chuckle, "but why are you back here? It's great to see you back, but I thought you were long gone, publishing books or making movies, or porn or whatever I heard you were doing out in California!"

"Porn?" I laughed at that one. "No, it's a lot easier to get into major movie acting than it is to get into porn. You have to be a really good writer or actor to get in that business, so I stuck with journalism, because porn is too hard." I jokingly replied. He walked around the front desk and shook my hand and gave me a hard slap on the back.

"What are you doing here, man?" I asked, not really knowing what to say back to him. Wondering if that was the right thing to say to a friend who used to beat up my college friends for having too much fun at the local bars.

"I've been working here ever since July!" he replied as he explained his situation. "I got clean of the drugs and the juice, cleaned my life up after a bad accident and started working here, after Chuck quit. - He's back working here again, but when he quit it opened up this job. So here I am, bro!"

"Good stuff." I said. "Wait, Chuck who? The Chuck I went to college with, from back in the day?"

"Yeah bro! He works here too. You'll see him he's around. I told him that I heard you started working here. He's around here somewhere, you'll catch him some time or another." Chad replied, still smiling as if he was looking at someone who had been given up for dead.

Although I did leave suddenly, without giving much warning except to my friends Mack, Ducky and Carp, everybody else kind of got left behind and I never got to say good bye to a plethora of friends before I left for Los Angeles. (like I said earlier, my undergrad college days and then my tenure in California were different stories, for a different day)

"Are you married, yet?" he asked.

"Nope, not yet." I replied. "I haven't quite found that girl of my dreams that I've been waiting to just show up in my life at my front door."

"Yeah, if only it happened that way!" he added with a chuckle.

"No kidding. Wouldn't that be nice?"

"Yeah, but that's not going to happen, bro. Not in this world!" he replied.

"What about you, Chad? Married yet?" I asked.

"Engaged!" he replied.

"That awesome, dude. Congratulations." I said with excitement.

"Yeah, I'm smoking more, drinking harder and broke as shit. I think I got this down. If this is anything like marriage then I'm already good at it!" he said jokingly - I think he was joking. I wasn't sure.

"Good stuff."

The front desk phone began ringing. Perfect timing because I didn't know what else to say to him.

After a few minutes he hung up. "There's a situation in 1104. Domestic dispute." he explained. "I'll call and have another person from security meet you at the condo."

"What do I do when I get there?" I asked.

"I guess however they trained you. Just do what they taught you. Bro." he answered.

"But they haven't really taught me anything." I replied. "They just gave me a tour, told me where to walk and put me to work."

"Damn, that sucks!" he said. "Well, another security officer is going to meet you. I guess just watch him and help him out with whatever he needs."

"Right. Yeah, I can do that. I can pretend to know what I'm doing." I said, getting a little nervous.

"If there ever was a good bullshitter, it was you, Abbott!" he said as I walked towards the elevators.

"Thanks, I think. I'm not sure how to take that." I replied, a little offended.

He just kept laughing as I got on the elevator and the door closed.

I got off the floor on the first floor, which was the floor above the main level. In some areas it was high off the ground and at other places, due to the rocks and slope of the ground, the first floor of residential condos were barely a few feet above the ground. In this situation it is important to remember this little fact.

As I stepped off the elevator into the long hall, I could see another security guard already knocking on the door.

"Hey, I'm Abbott." I said, introducing myself.

"Nice to meet you, buddy. I'm John." he replied between knocks on the door. "Security! Open the door please! Sugar Peak Security! I advise you to please open the door, or else we will unlock the door and come in!'

Finally the door began to open. Through the dark of the other side of the door we could see a figure emerge.

"What's the problem?" asked a skinny shirtless younger man as I could suddenly see that he had blood running down his face and looked to have a bottle stuck in his head.

"Holy shit!" I exclaimed. "My god man, what happened to your head?"

"Huh?" he replied.

"Sir, is that a beer bottle stuck in your head?!" John asked, astonished at the sight before our eyes.

"I don't know, dude, but my head hurts." he groggily answered.

John grabbed his communication radio. "Front Desk call 911. We have a man, early twenties with a head injury!" John said.

"My girlfriend found out that I had sex with her friend, like five times and then she hit me over the head with something." The dazed and wounded man mumbled as he stepped out into the hall.

"You have a beer bottle stuck in your - skull!" I exclaimed again, still in shock. "That's crazy man! We need to get you to the emergency room!"

"No, not without my girlfriend." he said.

"Where is she?" John asked as he stepped inside the condo.

"She's out on the balcony, I think. I'm not sure dude." he answered as he stumbled around.

"Sit down. Just have a seat and John will go get her." I said as I couldn't stop staring at his head.

In a moment John came back to the hall. "She's on the balcony and said she's going to jump if I come any closer."

"Don't let her jump, man! She's the most important thing in the world!" he cried, as I couldn't stop looking at his head wondering how in the hell she jammed a beer bottle into his skull, and much less how he was still walking around and talking, well, sort of.

"You, go on around outside and calm her down until the police and ambulance arrive and I'll stay with this guy." John said as he kneeled down to examine the drunken man's head.

"What am I supposed to say?" I asked frantically.

"Just keep her calm, you'll think of something. Now go!" he replied.

I ran down the hallway to the nearest staircase. It was only a flight or two of floors to the outside fire exit, but it felt like it was taking a long time. I ran outside and down the side of the building. I almost nailed my head on the concrete basin of some of the balconies as the slope of the ground slopped upwards, closer to the first floor of balconies.

Suddenly I saw a girl in red sweatpants and a blue tank top standing on a balcony railing. It suddenly occurred to me that she was only about ten feet off the ground from even the top of the balcony railing.

I looked up at her standing slightly above me on the railing.

Although it was only a few feet off the ground my adrenaline was still pumping and I didn't want to startle her.

"Get back, I'm warning you!" she exclaimed. "Get back or I'll jump!"

"Whoa, now." I replied as I backed up a little, not wanting to alarm her. "I'm just out here to check on you and make sure you don't do anything stupid."

"Stupid? Stupid!" she screamed. "Stupid is ever having dated that asshole in the first place! Stupid is trusting him AND my bff! Stupid is thinking I was going to live forever with him and have babies and be so fucking happy that I can't stand it! Stupid is what he did to me!"

"Okay, okay, just relax... I'm sorry." I replied calmly.

A breeze started to drift across us as her brown hair blew across her face. She was an attractive college-age girl who seemed as if life was over. The only problem for her about that was: she was only a few feet off the ground.

"You know," I started to say, looking for the right words, "I know it doesn't seem like it, but your boyfriend is very sorry for anything he has done to you. I can tell just by - looking at him that he regrets ever cheating on you."

"Fuck him and fuck her! They can both rot in Hell, happily ever-after!"

"Why don't you come down from there and we can talk about it." I said, gently.

"Fuck him!" she said again. She was very good at balancing on the railing of the balcony as she took time to pull her hair up and put it in a ponytail.

"Listen, you don't have to talk to him, but please just come down from there and I'll come inside and we can talk." I asked, again.

"What makes you think he gives a shit about me, or is even sorry at all? I hate him!" she replied.

"Well, for starters, he has a broken beer bottle stuck in his head like he just was in a Mexican bar fight." I answered, now getting somewhat annoyed wondering why in the hell the police hadn't arrived.

"Is he okay?" she whimpered as she began to cry and her eyes turned puffy and red.

"I don't know," I said calmly, "that depends on what he was like, before."

"He was a fucking idiot." she replied through her tears.

"Yeah, then in that case, he's fine." I shrugged.

"Did you know he's always checking out other girls and saying how he wished my boobs were bigger? Can you believe that? He's such a fucking asshole. I hate him!"

"Where are the damn police?" I said out loud as I looked around and listened for sirens.

"He cheated on me! With my best friend!" she cried. "And that's just the one I know about! There's no telling what other skank sluts he's banged. Fucking prick!"

"Can you believe that the one time you want the police to actually show up and they're not even here yet?" I said quietly to myself, not knowing if she heard me, but it was obvious she was caught up in the thought of her boyfriend having cheated on her with her best friend.

"Do you think I'm pretty? If you were dating me and I was very good to you, would you cheat on me?" she asked me as her tears began to slow down.

"Yeah, I think you're pretty. Without a doubt. Would I cheat on you? No, I wouldn't do that because -" I had to think quickly, "you don't deserve that. Nobody does. What you do deserve is someone a lot better than that piece of shit, but we all make mistakes and we learn from those mistakes."

"He was such a big fucking mistake!" she screamed, as she became hysterical. "I hate him! I hate him so much I'm glad I stabbed his dumb fucking head! He deserved it!"

"Yes, he did deserve it." I replied as I stepped closer, "now, will you come down off that balcony railing and talk to me?"

"No! Stay away from me! You don't care neither, you just want to get me off of here so you can go back to doing - whatever it is you're doing and not waste your precious time trying to keep me from jumping and killing myself!"

I looked down at the ground and then back at her. I was getting aggravated at this girl now. She was annoying me and I wanted to get this over with. She was drunk and in deep emotional pain, but she was also making an ass out of herself and drawing attention from the other guest at the resort.

'Please come down." I said.

"No! I'm going to jump!" she yelled.

"Ma'am, please, he is not worth it. Please just get down." I said.

"No! If you try anything, or take one step closer then I'm going to jump!"

That was it. I had had enough.

"If you're going to jump, then go ahead and jump already. You're like six feet off the ground! You might sprain your ankle or break your arm, but what makes you think that jumping from this height is going to kill you? My god, already! I'm trying to be nice. I'm sorry you're upset. That guy doesn't deserve you, but this isn't the answer! Have you not even noticed how close you are to the grass!? Go ahead. Jump! This way we can get this over with and you can ride with beer-head to the hospital and fix your neck or arm, whatever breaks when you hit the ground - if you even actually break anything!"

I would make a horrible psychiatrist or hostage negotiator.

"She looked stunned and shocked, not so much at what I said but at the fact she just realized she was only a few feet above the ground.

"Oh my god," she said astonished and humbled, "I'm such an idiot."

"No, no you're not." I replied, sternly. "You are just young, dumb, drunk and in love."

"Isn't being dumb the same as being an idiot?" she asked as she climbed down off the railing back onto her balcony floor.

"No," I answered, "you can learn things in life and not be dumb, but being an idiot is a life-long problem."

"My boyfriend, ex-boyfriend, is an idiot. I'm just dumb. Young, dumb, drunk - but not in love. Not anymore."

"Good for you." I replied. "See, you're already not nearly as dumb as you were yesterday. You learned you don't need to be with the guy with the beer bottle stuck in his skull. You deserve better."

"Thank you." she said through her drying tears and puffy red eyes.

Suddenly I could see the flash of emergency vehicles off in the near distance.

"No need to thank me." I replied.

"I'm going to go check on Seth." she added as she walked into her condo.

"What's your name?" I asked.

"Elizabeth." she answered. "It rhymes with Seth. Elizabeth and Seth."

"Yeah," I added, "but not everything that rhymes goes well together. There's a lot of crappy songs and bad poetry that rhymes."

"You're right." she said, showing a little smile and almost with a laugh. "Thanks, again. Hey, what's yours?"

"Call me Abbott."

"Abbott." she said as she thought of something that rhymed with my name. "Abbott...."

"Abbott!" I said beginning to rhyme, "Abbott, your boyfriend is a bad habit. So, listen to what I say - and stay away, from him. Don't do it, again!"

"Yeah," she said with a laugh, "him and I make bad poetry."

"I agree."

"Well, no matter, I better go check on him and make sure he's alright so I can kill him later."

"Have a better evening." I said as she walked inside.

I guess my job and my life wasn't completely useless at the moment. I mean, I did save a girl - from possibly spraining her ankle... by yelling at her.

CHAPTER 7:

BAR FOOD, POLICE CARS & PROBLEMS

When I got home that night a little after eleven in the evening, I managed to slip past crazy guy's door without being detected. When I stepped inside the first thing I wanted to do was have a snack before I went to bed. I was starving. Between the gate accident, the beer bottle-head incident and the 'jumper' ten feet up in the air, I had never taken time to eat that evening at work.

The refrigerator looked as if it had never been used. It was completely clean - of any food or drink. I rummaged in my cabinets only to find an empty cereal box, which had it been filled with delicious grain cereal I didn't have any milk to pour in the bowl along with any cereal, which I didn't have.

I decided to go back to the bar & grill where I had hung out some during my under-grad college days. I knew they served food until one o'clock in the morning so my chance of getting something to eat and a buzz before bed just went up by one-hundred percent.

When I arrived at my destination it brought back a few old memories of hanging out with my friends. Ox breaking his ankle sliding across a piss-covered bathroom floor, Mack walking through the door just in time to see his slutty girlfriend standing on top of the bar flashing everyone and then making out with another girl, who was also topless. They were banned from the bar for a year. Ducky, our skinny-hippie-ish black best friend, who wrangled his way into accidentally insulting a few of the bearded locals, and myself having to jump in and throw a few punches to help out so we could escape with our dignity and save our virgin heterosexual butt holes.

The nostalgic smell of alcohol, cheese fries and armpits filled my nose as I almost gagged and realized why I didn't eat actual food here at this place back in the day.

I oozed over to the bar and had a seat near the end. It looked like a nice quiet corner to enjoy a bite to eat and not feel awkward, in the middle, and out of place in a bar where I once could have gone and always known a dozen people in there on any given night. But now, it was a familiar setting with only strange new faces, and I too grabbed a couple of looks that asked 'who's this guy?' Another new face to town? Actually, my face suddenly did seem new as I realized that I felt like I was starting over new, in my old town.

"What can I get you?" the bartender asked, not saying 'Hey Abbott, long time, no see!' because this person had obviously never seen me before.

"Bacon cheese fries." I replied. "And a beer, please."

"Sure thing, bud."

To my left I noticed the classified section of a newspaper. I reached for it and began looking through the HELP WANTED page as I hoped there was something that might interest me more than what I was currently doing. Most jobs seemed to be for RN's, gas station attendants, and some for maid services at hotels. I guess, in a way, I was lucky to get my job as a security guard at the resort on the top of Sugar Peak when I did, or else I would have had to pretend to talk with a foreign accent and learn how to properly make a bed so I could be a maid, because I might have been educated but I wasn't a nurse. It seemed to be the only option left. There definitely weren't any career opportunities in journalism at the moment. Even screenplay and television writers were out of work at the moment because of the strike going on in Hollywood. I was beginning to think that maybe I should just give up on my dreams of being a journalist and writer all together. Between the two, my job on Sugar Peak Mountain definitely paid more at the moment, no matter how little it might be.

"Already looking for a new job? You just started!" Bo said from behind me.

"Hey, Bo." I said, surprised to see him here, "What are you doing here?"

"Just having a bite to eat and a beer before I go home." he said as he stood there making me feel uncomfortable as if he was waiting for me to invite him to sit next to me at the bar that clearly anyone could sit down at and have a drink or whatever.

"Uh, want to have a seat, man?" I asked.

"Yeah okay." he said with a bobble of his head and a smile. "Listen, I am really sorry, again, for dropping the gate arm on your car."

"Don't worry about it, Bo." I replied as my bacon cheese fries arrived and I became distracted by hunger as he continued to talk while I ate my bacon cheese fries and pretended as best I could to pretend that I was listening. He talked about, I think, his girlfriend, his job at the gatehouse, living in the mountains, blah blah, - blah blah. Who cares because I have bacon cheese fries and I am hungry and not listening. Blah blah.

Hey, Bo," I said, changing the topic, "did you know that French fries are the slutty food of the fast-food world? They're cheap, they are shared by two or more people, nobody actually wants them until they see them and then they can't resist. French fries are always around more French fries. They make you feel good, but then you pay for it in the long run and wish you never had them. Slutty fries you are so hard to resist! My will power is obliterated."

"So, what's your story?" he asked enthusiastically.

He seemed like a real nice, friendly guy, but all I could do was stare at him for a moment with bacon cheese fries hanging out of my stuffed mouth, realizing that I didn't hear anything he had said, but even more astonished that he wanted to know my story, which I didn't know where to begin or what to even say to him. Honestly, I just wanted to be left alone and wallow in self-pity with a beer, bacon cheese fries and relax. Then I felt bad, so I finished chewing and summed it up quickly, just giving him the cliff-notes.

"Okay, well...." I began to speak quickly. "I was a DJ at a radio station while I was a student at the university here in town. I graduated in only six years, had an awesome - fun time. Made great friends, learned important lessons about life, love and the pursuit of drunkenness. One night I was in a gas station with a friend, just down the road, getting a soft-drink and paying for gas when an asshole tried to rob the place. We scuffled, he hit his head and knocked himself out so I took a shit on his face to teach him a lesson, but a few days later he was out on bail and broke into my house, stabbed me with a knife and left me for dead. Grew up, made amends with friends, made new friends, moved away - drove to California to start my life over. Went back to school in Los Angeles for journalsim. Almost got killed by a suicidal jumper who fell twenty stories above my head - he landed six feet in front of me as I was walking home from class. Bodies don't look like they do on TV, you know, they splatter and bounce when they hit concrete, and that mess gets all over you like a water balloon. - So, I loaded up the car with everything I owned that could fit inside my crappy blue car and drove back here because I was going to work with a newspaper, but that fell apart and didn't happen so here I am! Working at the Peak of Sugar Mountain, as a fucking security guard!" I end with a smile.

He just looked at me dumbfounded and in shock. His fat little face was frozen and his eyes were wide and motionless.

"Well," I added, breaking the silence, "that's just the short version of it all. No reason to be specific. That sums up the back of the book, you could say..."

He still didn't move a muscle.

"My god, Bo. Say something! You're freaking me out. Are you having a medical issue?" I looked around. "Do I need to call for help? Bo?" he was freaking me out.

After a moment, he spoke.

"You took a shit on somebody's face?" he asked.

"He was a bad guy." I shrugged. "I just wanted to teach him a lesson about being too lazy to get a real job. I hoped it would make him reevaluate his life of crime." (read the prequel)

"You shit on a person's face?" he asked again, still in shock.

"Yeah, but I told you he was a very bad person. Hey, is that the only part you got out of everything I said? Did I lose you at that moment?"

"What?" he said, finally coming back to earth. "No, of course not. I heard everything. When I asked you about your 'story' I just never - never ever expected to hear something like that, at all!"

"And that's just the cliff-notes, Bo. It's better that way. You don't need to hear everything." I said as I went back to eating my bacon cheese fries and sipping on my beer.

"Hey," I added, looking at my beer, "how could you stick one of these in a person's head, anyways? I guess you break it first, but how is that physically possible?" I asked, thinking about the dude with the beer bottle stuck in his head.

"Huh?" he asked, confused.

"Oh, you didn't hear about that?" I asked as I put money on the bar for my meal and got up to leave.

"Abbott, you should write a book!" he exclaimed. "Wow, that was amazing! I mean, I know you summed it all up for me real fast, but holy crap! That is crazy! That would definitely be a good book!"

"Huh?" I shrugged as I thought about it for a second. "Nah, I don't know..."

"I would read that book! I don't even like to read!" he added enthusiastically.

"Well, thanks, Bo. I'll think about it." I said as I gave him a slap on the arm and walked away. "See you at work!"

"Yeah, see you at work, tomorrow! Later Abbott!"

"Later, man." I walked outside.

When I got in my blue piece of crap it wouldn't crank.

"Sounds about right." I said to myself as I locked it up and started walking. Nobody walks in the mountains; everything is either uphill or downhill. It's a lot like hiking except you're not dressed for hiking and you are the only idiot not in a car on the road and there's still that danger of bears, bobcats, and people lurking in the woods who were born without social security numbers because nobody knows they exist. At least I was sober enough to run away in a semi-straight line, if need to do so, on my way home.

As I walked the three or four miles towards my apartment I noticed the flashing of blue lights behind me.

"You there, walking!" said a voice over a loudspeaker from the police car. "Stop walking! Put your hands in the air where I can see them!"

I wasn't doing anything wrong, I turned to look.

"Don't turn around! He commanded. "Lift your shirt so that we can see you don't have any weapons!"

I lifted the back of my shirt.

"Now slowly turn around!"

I turned, slowly, I couldn't see due to the fact that the bright lights from police car were blinding me.

"I'm not drunk, I only had one beer." I yelled. "I'm not even driving. I'm just walking home. My car broke down."

"Quiet!" the voice said. "Turn back around and face the other way! Lift your arms out to the side! Move them up and down! Slowly... slowly! Up... and down. Up... and down."

What the hell is going on here? I wondered.

"Now drop your pants! Keep flapping your arms like a bird!"

"Drop my pants?" I yelled. "How am I supposed to drop my pants if I - what the hell?" I turned to look. This couldn't be real. It seemed more like something I would do to a friend.

Then I heard laughter.

"Abbott!" said a familiar voice as a figure stepped out of the passenger side "Abbott, I'm just messing with you. That was hilarious! I got you so good, dude!"

"Chuck? Chuck, is that you man?"

"Yeah, it's me! How have you been?" he laughed.

I ran over to the police car.

"Finally, Abbott fell for a prank that he himself couldn't do better!" Chuck said as I gave my old friend a hug.

"What's happening! How have you been?" I asked.

"I'm great. Get in!" Chuck replied. "We'll give you a ride home."

I climbed in the back of the police car.

"This is my friend, Max." Chuck said, introducing the officer. "He was on his way to drop me off at home, when we saw you walking. I couldn't help it man, sorry, but that shit was hilarious."

"Nice to meet you, Abbott." he said, still somewhat laughing, quietly.

"I told him you were cool and wouldn't tell on him for letting me do that." Chuck explained as we sped down the road.

"I've had my own cop car pranks back in the day." I said.

"Hey, you guys got a few minutes, or do you need to get on home?" Max asked.

"I got time," Chuck replied, "Jenny is visiting her parents for the next couple of days while I have to work, so I don't really care to go home to an empty house."

"Yeah, me too" I added. "My - nobody isn't there either, so whatever y'all wanna do."

"Cool." Max said as we turned down a small little side road in the woods. "There's an open field back here and when I get bored I like to do donuts in it."

"You're going to let us drive, right?" Chuck asked.

After a moment of regretful thought, Max replied, "Okay, just be careful. There's nothing out here, so I don't see why not. We can't really wreck the car in a flat field."

That's what he thought. Although, I knew that Murphy's Law was always waiting in the background to pounce if the opportunity arises.

"Here we go! Round one!" Max said as we turned off into the flat field and began tearing it up like the Duke Boys.

We turned and spun around and back up and gunned it forward. It sounded as if we had to be messing something up under the police car because I know we slightly bottomed-out quickly a few times during our escapade of being irresponsible in a responsible vehicle.

Chuck took his turn and scared the crap out of both of us, and then it was my turn. You see, this is when Murphy's Law kicked in: If something can go wrong, you can be sure it will (possibly... maybe... well, some of the times).

I gunned it as I turned to the right and then back to the left. Our frightened happy faces of thrills and terror.

BAM! CLUNK!

I had no idea what happened. It felt like I got punched in the face by a blow-up doll or a heavy over-sized beach ball.

I felt blood running down my lip. The airbag had deployed. It didn't look like we hit anything. It's not like I hit a tree, building, or - anything.

I looked over at Chuck, who was up front in the passenger seat, his airbag had also deployed, obviously. We just looked confused.

I turned to look in the backseat at Max to say sorry. I couldn't see him.

"Max, I'm sorry! I don't know what happened. Max... Max? Where's Max?"

"I'm down in the floor." he replied. "Because I am screwed!"

"I'm so sorry. I don't know what happened!" I said.

"All I know is," he begun to say, "is the pain from hitting the glass divider in front of my seat is going to be nothing compared to the pain I'm going to be in when I report this."

"What are you going to say?" I asked, quietly, still not knowing what happened, exactly.

"I have no idea." he mumbled from down in the floor of the backseat.

"Whatever we hit, it's gotta be under the car." Chuck said as he opened his door and stepped out.

I had to forcefully push on mine a moment and then it opened.

"Look underneath from your side." Chuck added.

"I can't, I'm pretty much bottomed-out over here." I replied.

"There's something sticking out on this side." Chuck said, as I walked over to the passenger side of the police car.

We shined our phone light under the car at what appeared to be a wagon wheel.

"What the -"

"Is that a wagon wheel?" I asked, dumbfounded.

"Where the hell did a wagon wheel come from?" Max asked as he got out of the back seat.

"Hey, I thought people in the back seat couldn't get out of a police car?" I asked.

"I don't know," Max mumbled and shrugged, "we don't arrest too many law-breakers around here, especially dangerous ones."

"That's a good question." Chuck added. "Where the hell did a wagon wheel come from?"

"From a - wagon." I replied, realizing in the middle of my sentence that I sounded like a smart-ass; and I happened to be the unlucky bastard who had the honor of running over said wagon wheel, causing the airbags to deploy and ending Max's career at the Sugar Mountain Police Department. I accidentally ruined someone's life after only knowing him for about thirty minutes. I think that was a new record for myself.

"Look," Chuck replied, "we have got to figure out what we're gonna do about this. We have to call somebody. We can't just leave it here."

"Yeah, it's not like it was - stolen." I added, as I soon thought of a great idea - well, an idea, if not the best, at least it was something. "Just report it stolen! You can say that you stepped out of your car to take a piss and somebody jumped in and drove off in it!"

"Nah, that'll never work." Max replied.

"Okay, then just tell them that you took two friends mud-slinging while on duty and you totaled it." I added.

"Let's report it stolen." Max quickly agreed. "I won't be in nearly as much trouble."

"Well, let's start walking." said Chuck. "We've got a long way to go."

So, we started walking.

"Who knows, maybe we'll get a ride." I said as we walked down the dark, lonely road through the woods.

"Well, we had one, and we blew it." Chuck added.

"Sounds about right." I said.

CHAPTER 8:

PICKING UP AN OLD PERSON CAN LIFT UP YOUR LIFE

"Have you ever been to that strip club called 'The Fruit Cups'? Bo said as we sat in the break room sipping on coffee and watching the television.

"Yeah, back in college." I replied.

"Have you ever seen that stripper-lady who does that thing with the celery stick and the pimento cheese?" Bo asked.

"Oh, yeah." I said. "Don't remind me. I don't want to think about that right now."

"Bo, shouldn't you be at the gate house?" John asked as he walked in the break room and sat down at the table.

"Farrell said he would watch the gates for me while I took a break." Bo replied as he munched down on a doughnut.

"Oh, no. No, Bo!" John said with a sigh.

"What?" Bo said with a mouth full of goodness.

"Bo, everybody knows that Farrell says those things and then walks away because he thinks it's funny and then he denies he ever said he would give someone a break. He doesn't know how to work the gates! He's messing with you man! You're going to get in a lot of trouble!"

Bo about choked on his doughnut as his eyes grew large and he stumbled out of his chair and ran out of the break room.

"I didn't know that. I do now, though. I'm glad that didn't happen to me." I said with a sigh of relief.

"I made all that up." John replied. "Bo is so easily fooled sometimes! That shit was hilarious!"

"Like I said, glad that wasn't me." I repeated as I went back to watching television. It was sort of funny, but I wasn't in the mood to laugh. I was tired from all that walking I did last night and I didn't feel like picking on someone who was easily manipulated and very nice. You had to fool somebody who thought they were smarter than you for it to be justified, otherwise it was just wrong.

"When is your break over?" John asked. "Got time to play ping-pong?"

"No thanks," I replied, "I don't play ping-pong, but I'm not on break. I just didn't feel like walking around and helping old ladies get across the parking lot to their cars. I'm tired."

"Oh. Are you not worried about getting in trouble?" he asked.

"What are they going to do? Fire me? Then I have to draw unemployment benefits and sit at home. I'm cool." I said as I ignored him and went back to watching TV.

"Okay, well, I didn't hear that." John said as he walked away.

"Thanks." I acknowledged.

Over the intercom I heard the front desk paging me to come to the lobby. I finished my coffee and then slowly walked to the front desk to see what they needed from me. I should have stayed hidden in the break room, because Hilary was working and nobody liked her. Seriously. She was a bitch. A fat one, too.

"Well, it's about time you got here!" Hilary squawked. "I told them that I had no idea where you were and that you probably weren't doing what you are supposed to be doing."

"What are you talking about, Hilary?" I asked, as anytime I had to deal with her it drained any small amounts of enthusiasm I might actually have had for my new job.

"God, you are such a weirdo." she said as she rolled her eyes.

"First of all, my name is not God, it's Abbott, but you're not the first girl to call me that. Secondly, out of everybody that works here how am I the weirdo?" I asked, having no clue what was wrong with her attitude, constantly. I really didn't care, but she insulted people like it was nothing, when most of the time she had no single cause to do so. It was absurd and stupid.

"Whoa, now!" she pathetically said. "Don't get all crazy on me tiger! I was just kidding around!"

"huh?"

"Scotty, in unit 1062, needs your help getting up. He says he's fine, but he fell and his wife is gone shopping -"

I didn't even let her finish talking. I punched the elevator button and headed up to his condo.

The door was unlocked. I walked in and yelled for him as so not to scare him.

"I'm in here!" he shouted. "Come on in Abbott, I'm in the master bedroom on the floor."

"Scotty, are you okay?" I asked as I grabbed hold of him and helped him to his feet.

"Yeah, I'm fine, I'm just getting older and older every day. I can't move around like I once could." he said as we walked into the living room and he sat down in his recliner. "Can you believe that I used to be a fighter pilot? Now they won't even let me drive a damn car. Sons of bitches. Can you believe that?"

"I'm sorry, Scotty." I said quietly.

"The other day the wife and I went for a drive out by Watauga

Lake. We had a small car accident. I didn't think I side-swiped the car but apparently I did. So, the next thing I know the DMV revoked my driver's license. I can't even go anywhere without my wife having to drive me. Do you know how embarrassing that is?"

"I'm sorry to hear that, Scotty. I hate that for you." I answered.

"Well, damn them. It was an accident, but they said I couldn't pass the test to keep my driving privileges. It's a damn shame. One day, you're high on your horse, earning the living as a U.S. Navy fighter pilot in the world's best Navy, and then the next you're a retired old fool who doesn't work, can't hardly walk around his own apartment and can't drive a goddamn car."

"Well, you wanna trade places!" I said, joking around. "Seems to me that not having to work and never worry about getting a DUI and being married to the woman of your dreams is the life." I hoped that made him feel a little better.

"Hey partner, I am smart enough to know that a guy like you, with the education that you have probably wouldn't be at a resort doing shitty work if he had any other choice. You're way over qualified for helping old people off the floor and carrying luggage and telling young people to quiet down and writing parking tickets - whatever the hell you do here, but enjoy it anyways! Enjoy it and be glad that you are young and have your health and your whole future ahead of you. I know you won't be here long, hell, everybody knows that! You are too damn good to be working here, doing what you do, all your whole life, but others aren't that fortunate, and they resent their jobs - before you know it they're old and have wasted there life complaining about how much life isn't fair. They fail to enjoy what they do have! I know you don't like your job. It's obvious, but accept it for now and know better things are coming soon. You'll see! Give it time."

"It's that obvious, huh?" I replied.

"Don't worry about it, Abbott. It's written all over your face. Hell, you never know, you might be General Manager of this place one day."

"I don't think I want to have to work here that long." I replied.

"Well, whatever you do-"

"Enjoy it." I finished the sentence for him and nodded as I clinched my teeth in thought.

"Speaking of 'shitty work', I have to go do some of my own." Scotty said as he stood up from his recliner and hobbled towards the bathroom.

"Just do me a favor and don't ask me to come help you get off the toilet!" I said as I walked to his front door. "You're nice to me, and I appreciate it, but I ain't helping anyone off the toilet. I had to help my grandpa one time get off the toilet and I never recovered. I still get memory smells from that event every now and then!"

Scotty laughed. "Well, thank God I only have war memories."

"Yeah," I replied, "You don't know how lucky you are!"

"Goddamn hilarious kid." Scotty said as he closed the bathroom door.

CHAPTER 9:

WHEN ONE DOOR CLOSES ANOTHER PIPE BUSTS OPEN

I t was a dark and stormy night on the television show that I was watching. It was 2:30 in the afternoon in reality and I had to be at work in thirty minutes. I stood in the mirror as I looked at myself in my security uniform. I had to pep-talk myself quietly every day before I went to work. It wasn't so much that I hated my job as it was the fact that I was doing nothing with my dreams and plans to be a writer, reporter, columnist or anything in that general field. Even in college when I worked at the radio station I didn't get paid more than peanuts but I loved my job. I knew that money wasn't the issue as much as just loving what I did and when you're already disappointed in yourself nothing can make it worse than having a job that was embarrassing. I never wanted to be seen in public in my security uniform in case I ran into someone I knew. I thought it would be humiliating and make me look like a complete failure, but as the days went by and time moved forward that embarrassing fear slowly began to fade as I accepted my current employment and tried to take Scotty's advice and enjoy life - no matter what I was doing, but it was easier said than done.

My phone began to ring. I didn't recognize the number but I answered it anyways.

"Hello."

"Hey, fucker!" Jake said on the other end.

"Jake! How's it going?" I replied.

"I got a new weapon yesterday. A semi-automatic rifle. It's pretty fucking sweet." he said enthusiastically.

"Oh," I said, "good stuff. Have you got to kill anything with it yet, or shoot stuff?"

"No, but I got to blow up some grenades for fun the other day at work. It was awesome." said Jake.

"Sounds scary."

"Nah, Jake added, "it wasn't scary for me because I was the one throwing them, but maybe for everyone else."

"I can see that." I replied.

"Hey," said Jake, as he toned down, "I wanted to let you know that I am coming up your way around Thanksgiving. I want you to meet Sophia before the wedding so I don't have to introduce your stupid ass for the first time at the wedding!"

"That's right man," I replied, "I almost forgot that you are getting married. Congratulations, again, bro."

"Thank you!" Jake said as he paused for a moment. "When is your crazy ass going to get married? You better find someone and settle down soon before people start calling you a faggot, faggot!" That was Jake's way of being funny.

"When I find the girl of my dreams and fall in love with her, I'll know. So far - not yet." I said as I glanced at the time. "Jake, I have to go, but I'll call you or you call me and we'll touch base and make sure you are still coming to visit."

"We still have plenty of time, fuck-tard. It's not even Thanksgiving yet, so we will get in touch again in a few weeks."

"Sounds a like a plan." I said. "Have a good one, Jake."

"You too, buddy." he said.

I put my phone in my pocket and put an airplane bottle of rum in my other pocket just in case it's one of those days at work. Come to think of it, I really hadn't been drinking very much lately, but the cigarette intake had slightly increased.

My phone rang again. It was work calling.

"Hello?"

"Are you on your way to work? We've got a bad leak on the sixth floor." John said.

"I'm on my way right now!" I said as I ran out of the door, forgetting to lock it on my way out.

I didn't drive fast - I didn't own the place and I was on time. I went through the main gate, with no incident, then the second gate opened for once without me having to talk to the lady in the intercom.

As I clocked in the old maintenance guy, Rocky, waved at me down the service entrance hallway. "Come with me!" he yelled, "we've got a bad one on the sixth floor!"

On the sixth floor we entered a condo at the end of the building, on the corner. Water was everywhere and so were employees as they rushed to clean up the water. It had leaked down to every condo unit below.

"A pipe in the wall going to the shower busted." Rocky said as he grabbed a vacuum hose and started sucking up the water.

It didn't really look like they needed me so I started to leave and do my usual security rounds. I decided to go check the hallways below to look for any other signs of a leak, just to be safe.

After I stopped on the fifth and fourth floor I walked down the staircase to the third floor.

As I rounded the corner I noticed an old lady sitting in a chair in the hallway. She looked at me and tried to force a smile, but I could tell she had been crying.

"Are you getting this leak under control, young man?" she asked through a forced smile.

"Yes ma'am. The maintenance workers are doing all they can to get this fixed as soon as possible - is there anything I can do for you, ma'am?" I said, wondering if she way okay.

"No, thank you." she replied.

I smiled and nodded as I started to walk away.

"Everything I own is now soaked. There was water everywhere." she said as I stopped and listened. "My bedroom took a lot of water. The ceiling fell and now I have a waterbed, I guess you could say. It wasn't - but it is now!" She still continued to try and smile.

"I'm very sorry." I said "I know that we will do what we can to clean it up quickly.

"My ceiling has to be replaced, and my mattress." she continued, "my husband and I bought that bed about ten years ago. We slept on it every night together, until he passed away a couple of months ago. We lived here full-time. Not like most of the other condo-owners who only come up here and there and for the summer. This was our home for almost twenty years."

She paused as she pulled a tissue out of her purse and wiped away a tear.

"There was so much water. I found a picture of him that was knocked off my nightstand floating in a few inches of water." she said, still trying to hold her composure. "It's all ruined - and now my memories of him seem to be gone too."

I didn't know what to say. It touched my heart to hear about her loss.

"I'm so sorry." I whispered.

She smiled again. "I'm old. Our only child died from cancer when she was only twenty-five. I hadn't really thought about it until now, but I don't know what would happen to all my pictures and special little trinkets that my husband gave me as gifts. Nobody really cares about them but me."

As I listened my heart sank in the water. So to speak.

"Front desk, to security, Abbott. Come in!" my radio blurted.

"This is Abbott. Go ahead front desk." I replied.

"Can you come to the front desk, please. We have a situation in the parking lot."

"10-4." I replied.

"Good luck, young man. Thank you for listening to me. I'm sorry, I didn't mean to burden you with my troubles." she said before I walked away.

"No, it was no problem. There's nothing to apologize for. I'm very sorry for everything that has happened to you." I shrugged not knowing what to say because I felt very bad for her. "I'm very sorry." I humbly added.

"Thank you." she said again.

"You know," I added, before leaving, "The things we have in this life are to keep us happy, comfortable and full of good memories so that we never forget, but when we get to Heaven I believe we're able to relive those wonderful, happy times over and over as if they're just now happening. Why else would they call it Heaven unless it was our most favorite moment and full of things that makes us happy. You'll still have everything forever, don't worry what will happen once you're gone, because 'here' won't matter anymore."

"Young man." she said as she stood up and held out her arms. I walked closer to her and she gave me a very heart-felt hug. "Thank you! Thank you so very much!"

I nodded my head and smiled. I walked down the hall and stepped into the elevator.

CHAPTER 10:

CRAZY GUY ACCIDENTALLY GETS ME STONED

I didn't lock my door when I left for work earlier in the day, and I soon remembered once I got home. No matter, there wasn't any crime in my neighborhood. I did have a few weird neighbors and I could hear a few couples arguing every now and then and the feint sound of car speakers blasting everything from 70's rock to the newest rap music, but nothing that ever really made me concerned for my safety, until 'crazy guy' freaked me out with an accidental wild few hours; whom we will now use as his 'unofficial' name in caps, like any other name: Crazy Guy.

My front door was slightly opened when I walked in that night after staying a little late because I helped clean up the leak that damaged at least six condos on six different floors. That's when I remembered I didn't lock my door, but I was in somewhat of a hurry to get to work after John called to tell me about the leaks.

Something felt strange, but as I looked around at the organized mess in the living room, and kitchen, I knew that even if someone had entered my apartment they would quickly leave because the fun of ransacking an apartment and taking valuables was not an option when it was my place. I had already ransacked it myself little by little over the past few months and the most valuable thing in my apartment was a half-emptied $50 bottle of expensive rum that I had borrowed from the restaurant at the resort. Sometimes people used the word 'borrowed' out of context, but I actually planned to return it once I had finished the bottle.

There was an odd smell. I didn't smell it right away, but after about a minute it filled my nasal cavities as it made my head feel dense. It wasn't the stove or the oven. I didn't leave burnt popcorn in the microwave and I double checked my own clothes and armpits just to make sure. Although, it wasn't so much a bodily smell as it was a feint smoke-smell.

Suddenly, I heard a splash-clunk noise in the bathroom, as if something had been dropped into water.

Maybe I was hearing things after being around water all day, but I slowly walked over to the bathroom door and opened it.

A cloud of smoke attacked me before I could even step into the bathroom. Through the haze I could see someone sitting in my tub. I startled them as much as they startled me. I fell backwards and ran into the kitchen as I frantically began opening drawers looking for a knife. Three drawers later I still couldn't find one. This was absurd. Did I not own any knives? I did, but for some reason I couldn't remember that they were in the dishwasher. I grabbed a fork and then suddenly realized that with the right poke I could hurt the intruder bathing in my tub and smoking some sort of drug in my bathroom because he was naked. A fork can hurt skin. Maybe. I didn't have a choice because the fork was all that I could find.

"Don't shoot! Don't shoot!" the intruder yelled as he ran into the living room. It was Crazy Guy and he was naked. That was even scarier than finding him in my bath tub unexpectedly. "Don't shoot me dude!"

I held the fork up towards his torso. "I will if I have too!" I yelled out of shock and fright. How I was supposed to be able to shoot him with a fork was unknown to me, but as long as he thought I had a gun I felt better about the situation, as if I had the upper hand in the matter.

"What the hell are you doing here, in my apartment?!" I yelled, still holding him at fork-point.

"Huh...." he thought about it.

"What the hell are you doing taking a bath in my house? And what are you smoking... it ... it smells weird, man. Like... like..." it was beginning to affect my senses. "What is that? What are you... Doing here, man?"

"I know were friends-" he said in a jittery-nervous voice. "I just thought since you were gone I could take a bath here. My water is cut off and I can't take a bath without water. You need water to take a bath and I thought 'well, I'll be gone before he comes back home...' so I used your water. Water is water. It doesn't cost much."

"First of all, dude, go back in the bathroom! You're naked! In my house!" I yelled.

"Oh, sorry!" he blurted as he ran back into the bathroom.

"And," I continued, "how would I not notice you were here when my apartment smells like... like... what the hell is that?"

"It's a little weed mixed with angel dust and some other stuff, like acid, I picked up in Canada last year." he answered from the bathroom.

I blinked my eyes a few times as I knew there was enough smoke in my apartment to start affecting me by second-hand drug smoke. "Holy shit, Crazy Guy, how much did you smoke?"

"All of it." he replied, "Well, most of it. I dropped my bowl in the tub right before you interrupted my bath, man." he answered as he walked out in my bath robe.

"Why are you wearing my robe?" I asked, annoyed, as I still held the fork out at him.

"Be careful where you point that thing! It could go off man! You could break something in here, or worse, you could accidentally shoot me!" he stuttered as he put his hands up in the air to show he wasn't packing any forks of his own.

"Oh, it won't be an accident if you don't get your shit - and... and - leave, soon...." I started to feel the effect of all the different drugs floating in the air.

"I think I might have smoked opium, man. I can't remember?" he added as he turned to walk back in my bathroom.

"Stay where I can see you!" I exclaimed. "Don't move or else I'm not afraid to use this... this... this is a fork?"

"No, that's a pistol, man. I know a pistol when I see one," he replied as he pointed nervously, "and that's definitely a pistol-fork!"

"Did you say it's a pistol or a fork?" I asked. I was feeling weird.

"A fork? That's not a fork man." he said, as he pulled on his hair and wiped his hand on my robe, acting freaked-out as usual, except he was looking weirder than usual. Everything was looking and feeling weird.

"You're right," I replied, "That's not a fork. It's a pistol. It's a - a fistol! No, wait! It's a - spork! - Pisork!" I, for some reason, found that funny, even though I wanted Crazy Guy out of my apartment.

"That's not a spork! Sporks are plastic and they look like spoons, but there not spoons! There forks shaped like spoons! You don't know what you picked up until you get some applesauce and then go to put in in your mouth and cut your tongue on the fork!" Crazy Guy said as he would take a few steps closer and then get freaked out and back up a couple of steps.

"Sorry, Crazy Guy, but you have to leave, because you broke into my home and took a bath in my living room and smoked a mixture of only God knows what, man." I said as I was astonished at his innocent intrusion, yet I was freaked-out myself for having my tub and robe violated.

"I didn't take a bath in your living room, that's impossible!" he replied.

"After what I saw today at work, you'd be surprised at where you can take a bath, and do cannonballs. It's possible to bathe, swim or do the backstroke in a living room." I said, still pointing the fork at him, somewhat.

"You're weird, dude." he said.

Crazy guy gathered up his clothes and walked to my front door.

"Thanks for letting me use your bathroom, but I have to be honest," he said, "you are a little strange!"

"Me?" I said, somewhat giggly, "Me? You think I am strange?"

"Yeah," he replied as he opened my door. "a little."

I closed the door behind him and locked it.

It was bright so I put my sunglasses on and lit a cigarette as I stared across the room and thought about how insulting it was that, of all people, Crazy Guy actually thought I was a little strange. I looked at my reflection in the window and noticed how loopy, twirly, and colorful I looked. I appeared to have on three pairs of sunglasses and a cigarette in my mouth.

"Okay, I'll accept that. I do look a little weird." I said to myself as I put my cigarette in the sink and then floated over to my bedroom and fell on the bed.

The next thing I knew I was walking and dancing to the sounds of disco as everybody from work appeared through the clouds.

Rocky, the old maintenance man, was there with a flame-thrower that shot out bunnies and pot leaves while everyone danced around and grabbed a bunny. I saw big fat Hilary and pushed her off the edge of the cloud. Everybody smiled and danced down the street of clouds to bikini-clad women in the distance.

"Where's the girl?" Chad asked.

"What girl?" I asked.

"Where's the girl?" Jerry asked.

"Which girl are you talking about?" I asked again, still smiling and dancing down the road.

"Where is the girl of your dreams?" Chuck asked. "Where is the girl of your dreams? The girl of your dreams isn't in your dreams!"

"That's probably because I don't know who she is, yet, but I'll find her!" I replied, happily.

"I won't drop the gate on your car again!' Bo said enthusiastically, but a girl is about to drop into your life very soon!"

Sunflowers began falling from the sky as I stood still and reached out my arms and smiled as they fell down around me.

One sunflower hit me in the face and it hurt as if I was punched it the face.

I woke up and was lying face down on the floor, realizing that the pain on my face was from falling out of my bed.

I laid there as I didn't feel like moving. I felt bad and heavy. I started to get angry at the thought of Crazy Guy violating my mental sanity, what was left of it, after ruining my tub and my bath robe. He could keep the bath robe.

I moved on past that thought and began to think about my weird dream and what my 'dream girl' and sunflowers had to do with my subconscious. I was feeling a little lonely, and knowing that my dream girl, whomever that was, wasn't even in my dreams made me feel that the one I was meant to be with may never show up at my door.

I farted; it made me feel better. I drifted back to sleep.

CHAPTER 11:

MY DAD, THE SMART-ASS DEMENTIA PATIENT.

I woke up and staggered to the kitchen where I downed one cup of water after another. I walked outside to stretch and enjoy the afternoon sunshine. It was a nice warm day in October as I realized my birthday was coming up. I didn't have to work today, so after I picked up my car from the mechanic, I decided to drive down to my hometown a few hours away and visit my dad in the nursing home.

A few hours later when I arrived at the nursing home I signed in at the desk and walked down the hallway to the lock-down ward. My dad had earned a spot in the secure wing of the nursing home after throwing a few temper-tantrums and a couple of foiled escape attempts. So now he had a nice room with a corner view of the woods in the escape-proof part of the nursing home.

My dad once weighed over 200 pounds and now he had been reduced to barely over half that weight. He had lost his will to eat and live, but God wasn't ready to take him yet - and although it might have been selfish of me to think this way: I was glad to still have him around, even though I know he was suffering mentally. I wasn't ready to give my dad away to the pages of family history and reduce him even further to just memories. I needed him in this world, for the sake of still having some family around. He could barely get out of his wheelchair only to climb in his bed or to sit on the toilet. His mind was mentally with 'it' on some days, more than others, and usually always somewhat grouchy, but never directly towards me.

When the nurse's aide opened the door for me he was waiting in his wheelchair on the other side of the hallway door. Right away I knew this was a good day for him because he was mentally competent enough to meet me when the office called to tell him that I was here to visit him.

"Hey there son!" he said looking up at me from his wheelchair. "You been enjoying the fast food? Kind of look like you've put on a few pounds."

"Hey pops." I replied "You look good. How have you been?" I was very happy to see him, as always, because I never knew when the last visit would be the last visit.

"I drew some pictures of what I thought about everybody in this place, and I stapled them to the walls. I got in a little trouble for that one." he said as he wheeled himself down the hall and I walked next to him.

"What did you draw, pops?" I asked, curiously.

"I didn't get in trouble for drawing," he replied, "I got in trouble for stapling them to the wall!"

"Oh, yeah, I can imagine that." I said as we slowly went down the hall towards his room.

"Well, it ain't like I didn't draw anything that wasn't true." he explained, "I might shouldn't have put everybody's name on their picture. Now, Mrs. Big-Butt knows that I call her "Big-Butt".

"Is her name really Big-Butt?" I asked.

"No." he looked at me like I was an idiot. "It's Gracie, but I drew a picture of her with a big butt, 'cause she's got one and then put her name at the top."

"Good God, pops. Why would you do that?" I asked.

"Because it's true! I was bored." he said as if it made perfect sense. "And now Patty knows she's got big feet. Hiding those things in fluffy slippers isn't fooling anybody! That old woman has got some big feet!"

I sighed. "How's everything else, pops?"

"Good."

"I'm glad to hear that." I replied as we turned to the left to go just a few more yards to his room.

"Oh! Oh!" a lady in a night gown screamed. "Oh, you ran over my foot! You ran over my foot! Ooowwww!"

"Well, if your big damn feet weren't in the way then I wouldn't have run over them! Now would I?" my dad growled.

"Are you okay, ma'am?" I asked, reaching out to help her.

"Leave me alone, you devil!" she screamed as she quickly hobbled away. "Leave me alone!"

"Dad, did you really just accidentally run over her foot, or is she just one of those-" I stopped, not wanting to insult anyone because my dad also was technically 'one of those - crazy people'.

"I told you she has big feet! They're unnatural." he said as we entered his room. "Talk about coincidence! We were just talking about her and those damn ugly fuzzy house slippers. You see, she's got big feet. Just pray you don't run into Big-Butt while you're here. You might not want to ever come back to visit your old dad!"

"That'll never happen." I laughed.

"So how's your new job at the paper? Are you enjoying it?" he asked.

Now, this is important to tell you: I hadn't told my dad that I wasn't working at the paper and had to settle for a crappy paying job as a security officer, because I knew he was proud of me and I didn't want to disappoint him in his final years, months or however much time he had left on earth. It wasn't so much to impress him as much as it was for his own pride.

"Things at work are a lot different than I ever imagined,' I replied, "but I have made some new friends and I never know what to expect."

"That's great!" he said as he moved from his wheelchair to his recliner. "I'm so happy to hear that you are happy. That's good news, son. I'm very proud of you."

"Thanks." I said, feeling bad about it, but it wasn't for me, it was for him and that made me feel better about not telling him the truth. I knew I was going to be a writer one day, and hopefully a journalist or even a columnist, just not yet.

"So, how have you been, son!" my dad said gleefully, "it's great to see you!"

"I'm good, Dad." I answered with a smile.

"You know, your mom hasn't come to see me in a while." he said as his tone changed. "I don't know why... she's probably busy. No -wait I think she came to see me last night. Yeah, well, sometime, she was here not long ago, but I haven't seen here today. Maybe she'll come soon."

"Dad -" I stopped myself.

"Where's your mom been, son?" he asked somberly.

I didn't want to have to tell him that my mom, his wife, was dead, and had been. His good day was starting to go away.

"Dad, I'm sure Mom will be here soon."

"Is she not with you?" he asked.

"No, pops. She's not here."

"Well, maybe she'll be here soon." he added.

One of the nurses walked in to give my dad his medication.

"This is one of my favorite nurses!' my dad said as he grabbed the little paper cup with the pills in it. 'She takes good care of me."

'Hello!" she said. "Now, take your medication. I'll see you again in a few hours!"

"Wait before you leave, let me introduce you to my son! This is my boy, Charles, he's going to college in the Fall."

"Nice to meet you." she said.

I shook my head discreetly to let her know I wasn't going to college. "Hey, nice to meet you, too."

"Yeah, my boy is going to college. His mother is going to be sad to see him go away, but that's what children do. They grow up!" he said as he turned on his television with the remote.

"I have to go, Pops, but I love you and I had a great time visiting with you this afternoon."

"Yeah, boy! We got to spend all day together, right?" he said as it sounded more like a question, as if he wasn't sure.

"We had a great time, pops. Thank you." I replied, trying to smile and not let it bother me.

"Good!" he said with a smile. 'It's always great to see my boy."

"And it's always great to see my dad." I replied as I leaned down to his chair and gave him a hug.

I walked out into the hallway and closed the door behind me. I leaned up on the wall for a moment to keep my composure.

"Are you leaving, young man?" a nurse asked.

"Yes, I am." I answered

"Okay, I'll let you out of the door." she replied as I followed her to the locked door that leads back to the main building.

"Hey, is there any way, just curious, that I can have a code to the door?" I asked.

"No," she replied, "I'm sorry, but I can't do that. We can't risk anyone giving the door code to one of our patients. It's the rules."

"I understand, no problem. I just thought it was worth a shot. It's a lot easier than waiting for someone to let me in and out."

"We're sorry for the inconvenience, but it is our policy." she added.

"Like I said, not a problem. I completely understand." I replied as she opened the door and I walked away.

That was always the hardest part - walking away. I never knew when it might be my last visit.

CHAPTER 12:

CHIPMUNKY BUSINESS

I was standing in the lobby at a distance listening to Hilary tell one of the Board of Directors members that she would have maintenance come change the light bulbs in their condo if she could get anyone to actually do anything.

"You can't ever find one when you need one!" she said, "they walk around and act like they're busy but they don't ever do anything. If it wasn't for me keeping all these morons in line it would be a disaster."

"Thank you for all you do, Hilary." he said, as if he meant it and didn't know any better.

"Oh, you're welcome!" she replied, "and F.Y.I. maybe you can do something about our security officers. They are just lazy! You might want to think about firing all of them and starting over. Just saying."

"Really?" he said.

She shrugged and smiled.

"I'll keep that in mind." he added as he walked away.

She looked over at me as I walked towards the front desk and rolled her eyes.

"I don't have any drugs or alcohol, vagrant, go away." she said.

"Well damn, that must really suck for you. How the hell are you going to make it the rest of the day, Hilary?" I replied.

She wasn't expecting to have anyone talk back to her so quickly. I think most of the other employees were so stunned by her comments or scared that she might eat them or sit on them that they were too afraid to say anything or just didn't know what to say back to her, because of being shocked by her bitchy remarks.

"Oh!" she gasped.

"I don't do drugs, Hilary, well, except for the other night - and that wasn't by choice." I said, referring to my mishap with Crazy Guy. "and I like to indulge in the occasional drink, but you, on the other hand, smell like beer every time you open your mouth. It's strong. I promise. I can smell it."

"I'm reporting you to Mr. Spacey and the board! You can't talk to me that way!"

"Go ahead," I responded, "Just don't stand too close or else they'll smell your breath. And maybe you should switch to light beer? I don't know - just a suggestion." I smiled as I walked away to do my hall walks to check each floor to make sure everything was fine.

"You are going to regret talking to me like that!" she yelled.

I turned around to smile and wave as I said, "Call me on the radio if you need me!"

"I'm reporting you immediately!" she screamed.

I noticed people walking in the lobby, so in order to avoid being bad-mouthed I fired the first shot in front of people, to avoid them believing what she might tell them.

"Hilary, I told you I'm sorry, but I can't go out with you! I have a girlfriend and I don't need two more - uh - one more, I'm sorry! It just wouldn't work. I like hygiene and that was a sweet idea but I think going to an AA meeting is something you need to do on your own, I can support you through prayer but I can't be with you. I'm glad you want to go to AA. That's a big step. I hope you can stay sober now. I'll be praying for you!" I tried to keep a serious, caring, and sincere face and not laugh until I stepped into the elevator and the door closed.

I got off on the 10th floor and almost slammed right into Jerry. He was one of the nicest people you would ever meet, but he looked a little frightening with one blind eye, built like a wrestler and had wild gray hair and a beard.

"Hey, where you going?" he asked.

"Just walking up and down the halls." I replied.

"Come with me." he said as he grabbed my arm and we stepped onto the elevator.

As we rode the elevator down towards the lobby it was silent. Jerry kept looking at the floor numbers as we traveled down past each floor. He was holding a broom in one hand and a plastic bucket in the other. He didn't say anything. It was an awkward silence as I wanted to ask where we were going and what we were doing, but I was a little afraid. I felt like I was about to get 'whacked' like in one of those mob movies. Even though he was a nice guy, like I mentioned earlier, he let out a persona of being kind of scary.

"Where are we going?" I asked.

"I need your help with something real quick." he answered.

"What are we doing?"

"I'll tell you in a minute." he replied, "We have to go to one of the conference rooms where some of the old ladies are playing cards."

"To do what?" I asked nervously.

He just looked at me for a slow second or two with that one good eye and then turned back to stare at the elevator numbers.

We stepped off the elevator and had to walk past the front desk before turning a left and walking down the hall to the conference / banquet rooms.

I looked at Hilary and waved with a slightly goofy smile and she glared back at me. I felt as if I had put a stop to her false bitching, at least with me.

We stopped at the door.

"We're about to go in here." he said quietly, "these women are scared to death."

"Why? What's going on?" I asked.

"There's a chipmunk in here and I bet'cha they're all standing on their chairs or the tables!" Jerry explained as he started laughing, "I didn't want to tell you what we were doing because I didn't want you to come up with an excuse why you couldn't help me like everybody else did!"

"Seriously?" I sighed.

"Yeah!"

"Alright, well, let's get this over with before I change my mind." I replied.

We opened the door. It was completely silent. Just like Jerry had predicted, all the old ladies were standing on their chairs or sitting on the tables except for one who didn't look like she had a clue what was going on, much less where she was at the moment.

"We last saw him scurry under the door of that closet!" a lady said as they looked scared, but happy to see us arrive to rid the room of the chipmunk.

"Open that closet door and when he comes out I'll beat him and scoop him up in this bucket." said Jerry as we moved toward the closet.

I heard a thump and looked to see that one of the ladies had passed out.

"Don't worry, she'll be alright." Jerry said as he assumed the position of a Spartan Warrior's stance a with broom in one hand and the bucket in the other hand.

"Whooo-ah!" I yelled. I couldn't resist. It looked like a rejected scene from the movie '300'.

"Open the door!" Jerry yelled.

Nothing happened. There were only a couple of metal folding chairs and a vacuum cleaner.

"Oh my God, Helen! Don't move!" a lady squealed to the other lady whom seemed to be completely mentally blank.

Helen just smiled, "Are we having banana pudding now?"

"We're going to have chipmunk soup!" Jerry yelled as he reared back in the mist of excitement and swung the broom to gentle brush the chipmunk off of Helen's back.

It didn't work out that way.

Helen took a broom to the back of the head and fell out of the chair.

"Damn!" Jerry growled as he started to chase it around the room.

Women screamed. I think a few more passed out. The survivors climbed down from their tables and chairs and hurried out of the conference room, as fast as senior-citizen ladies can move, in a disorderly fashion.

"Sum-bitch!" Jerry exclaimed as I could see him whacking the floor with the broom as if he was playing the 'whack-a-mole' game as you would find conveniently located at your local arcade or carnival.

Something this comical is hard to describe in a story, and can only really truly be funny if you could have witnessed it in person, or perhaps in a movie or TV show, but I was so busy laughing that I had given myself a pain in my side and could help Jerry try to catch the little chipmunk bastard.

Jerry was running around, swinging and smashing the broom, throwing the bucket and stomping, rolling and dancing all over the room.

I did take a second to wonder if this pain in my side was from laughter or was I having an appendicitis, but decided it didn't really matter.

The pain went away after Jerry trapped the frightened little chipmunk in the bucket. It wasn't an appendicitis.

"I've got him trapped under this bucket, but I don't know how to move it without him getting away!" Jerry pondered.

I walked over to see the plastic bucket turned upside down on the floor.

"So, what do we do know?" I asked, as I tried to catch my breath.

"Hell if I know!" Jerry said with a shrug.

"Hmmmm...."

Hilary never put a padlock on her work locker.

CHAPTER 13:

DING-DONG THE BOSS IS DEAD

Donald Spacey was a good boss. He was fair, yet firm. He told corny jokes all the time, but we all laughed for three reasons: 1. Some were actually funny. 2. He was the boss. 3. He would always get so tickled at his own jokes, even if he told them a dozen times a day. The fact that he laughed so hard at every joke he told, no matter how many times he would tell people the same joke, was the funniest part. He would laugh to the point of turning red in the face and his eyes would squint as he wheezed and coughed himself to death.

My boss, Donald Spacey, died on a Wednesday morning around 9 a.m. while telling a joke to a couple resort members. He had a heart attack and was dead before he hit the floor.

Suddenly we were left without a General Manager, a great boss and a good friend to many…. I mean, I didn't know him very well, but that is what the other employees said - that he was a great boss.

I felt obligated to go to the funeral. It was in the morning on the following Monday so I was able to go before I had to be at work later that afternoon. I wasn't really sure what to wear so I pulled out my old dark suite that I hadn't put on since my mother's funeral.

I walked in the church just a moment before it was to begin. I noticed Chuck, his girlfriend Jenny; Chad and his girlfriend Sarah; John and Bo all sitting near each other.

Dude, dude!" Chad said loudly as he motioned for me to sit next to him, "Over here!"

"Hey, how's everybody?" I said, greeting the group.

"Can you believe this?" Chad said in a loud whisper. "Donald dropped dead while telling a joke. That's crazy. One minute he's telling somebody about a Rabbi and a Priest and the next thing you know the fucker drops dead. BAM! Hits the floor like one of those old ladies in the Life-Alert commercials. Except he wasn't getting up."

"Ssshhhhh!" someone shushed him a few rows back.

"I'm just saying," Chad continued, "that shit is scary! It could happen to anyone us! At any time! Hell, somebody could drop dead right here during this funeral... you never know, dude. You never know."

"Sssshhhhhhh!" someone shushed him louder.

"Sorry," he replied, "I didn't mean to say 'hell'. Just think about it. Right here. In church. It's fucked up."

I should have just ignored him, but I found myself looking around, wondering if it did happen, and somebody did just drop dead right this moment, whom it would be.

"I doubt it, but you are right... You never know, but I hope not." I replied.

"I bet it would be Bo." Chad added. "Have you ever seen him eat? Big boy can put away a cheeseburger like it's a - a-"

"A cheeseburger." I said, finishing his stumped sentence.

"No," he added shaking his head, "you can't compare a

cheeseburger to itself. That doesn't make any sense."

"Why not?" I asked.

"There's a rule or something about that - you're not supposed to do that." Chad replied.

"Hey!" Bo whispered loudly from a few seats away from us, "Do you know that I can hear you?"

"Imagine that. He can't hear a fucking dump truck driving up to the gate, but he can hear me whispering about a cheeseburger." Chad said, astonished.

I just rolled my eyes and shook my head.

"I wonder who's going to sign our paychecks next week." John pondered.

"What the hell is wrong with you, dude?" Chad said. "A man is dead. Our boss is dead. Show a little respect, will ya? God!"

Everybody else was as stunned as John, considering John had a good point and was quiet about it and Chad was a little loud.

I raised an eyebrow as I thought about it for a moment.

"He's got a point," I said, "who is going to be our new boss? Somebody has to either get promoted or hired."

"And it's gotta happen soon," Chuck added, "because only the GM can sign off on a lot of the day to day business. Including paychecks."

"I thought you could do some of that stuff now?" Jenny asked.

"Yeah, baby, but with his authority. When we get a new boss he might change everything or start cleaning house." Chuck replied.

"What does cleaning his house have to do with our paychecks?" Chad asked, seriously.

"Uh, the new boss might fire everybody and bring in his, or her, own people. So, it technically has a lot to do with our paychecks." I explained.

"What the hell did I do to the new boss to get fired!?" Chad blurted.

"Sssshhhhhh!" someone shushed him again.

"Why does someone keep shushing me? That's rude, dude. This is a matter of life and death. I'm trying to talk about something important and this wise ass back here is trying to tell me to shush it."

"Nobody is fired, yet." I said, "But if he, or she, is in here right now I'm sure you're giving them a reason. We all are."

"What if the new Boss finds out that I dropped the gate on a few cars this year?" Bo worried. "What if they find out I dropped it on your car, Abbott?"

"You dropped the gate on Abbott's piece of shit?" Chuck asked, trying not to laugh."

"Abbott, I thought you said you wouldn't tell anybody about that?" Bo said, frantically, but quietly. We were at a funeral, you know.

"I didn't, Bo. You just did." I replied, getting annoyed. "Why is everybody acting like they've lost their mind? What the hell is wrong with you people?"

"Maybe Hilary will get fired." Chad said, "I hate her, she's such a bitch."

"I know, right." John replied.

"That would be nice." Chuck added, "But that's not going to happen."

"Why not? Chad asked. "How do you know? Can't you fire people, Chuck?"

"Only people in my department. I can't fire her without the Boss agreeing to it, and well, he's dead."

"How do you know that's not going to happen?" John asked as we all sank with disappointment at the idea of seeing Hilary over and over for as long as we worked at the resort.

"See, this is a perfect example of life being unfair." Chuck explained "We all prayed and hoped that Hilary would quit, get fired or die and then, out of nowhere, Mr. Spacey dies and Hilary's fat as keeps on trucking as if to rub it in our face that she's not going anywhere. Not yet."

"I don't think she's going to bother me anymore," I added. "I made it clear that every time she insults me that I'm going to embarrass her. Every time."

"Yeah, why is she such a - a - mean bitch all the time?" Chad blurted?

Everybody shrugged.

"Probably because she can't drink at work." I replied. "it's obvious she's an alcoholic.

"Yeah," Chad said, "when she sweats you can smell the alcohol emanating from her pudgy skin."

"That's nasty." I said.

"True Story." he added.

"Uh-oh," I said regretfully, "now I feel bad because I was making fun of her by telling her I couldn't go to AA meetings with her. I made it all up to humiliate her for being mean to me because people were standing nearby. She pissed me off, but now I feel bad about it."

"What we should do is fight for our right to keep our jobs. We need to organize!" Chad exclaimed.

"Organize?" John said, "Like a union? Yeah, that won't happen."

"What we need to do is fight stupidity in this country before we can even begin to fight for anything else. An increase in the literacy rate doesn't improve anything, it only increases the number of idiots who can read." I said with a growl, thinking of all the idiots I had come across in my life. It was a random thought, but my emotions were getting the best of me.

"Sssshhhhh!" somebody just shushed me.

I turned around to get a glance at whoever had shushed me. It was Hilary a few rows back. She glared and mouthed to me, "GO, TO. HELL."

"I'm not going anywhere with you." I said in a normal voice and then smiled.

"Oh!" she gasped in shock.

"My god, man…. We're all gonna be fired!" I said as I turned back around to face the front and shook my head as I slouched down in my seat.

CHAPTER 14:

BAD RUMORS THAT SWELL AND RISE

After work that night I went with a few people from work to a bar across the other side of the mountain to have a few drinks in honor of our departed boss, Mr. Donald Spacey. Chuck and Jenny were there, along with Bo, John, Chad, Jerry, and a few others.

"Here's to you, here's to me, but when it comes to death, damn that's about as shitty as it can be!" Jerry growled as he turned up his pitcher of beer and didn't stop until it was all gone.

I started thinking about what he said, and if I had to work at my current job all my life, death didn't seem that bad, actually, in a sarcastic way.

"Here's to one of the best bosses, ever." Chuck said.

"Here's to him giving me a job when I needed one!" John added.

"Here's to Mr. Spacey not firing me for all the times I could have been fired for my mistakes!" Bo said.

I hadn't known our deceased boss but for only a about a month, so I wasn't really sure what to say.

"I put the chipmunk Jerry caught in Hilary's over-sized pocket book be-fore she left work! So here's to - that!" I said.

Everybody got quiet for a moment and then shrugged and went

along to with it.

"Way to go, Abbott!" they yelled, and other stuff such as "Here's to that!" and "Why not!" or whatever, something like those sentences.

"I wonder what happened when she opened her bag?" I pondered, trying not to laugh.

We all imagined different ways of her being scared shitless when a harmless little chipmunk jumped out. It wasn't animal cruelty, for all of you who disapprove, I put some nuts in her bag - well, having to deal with Hilary might have been border-line cruel, but besides that, I didn't see the difference between keeping it as a pet in a cage or putting it in a pocket book for just an hour.

"I hope she didn't open it while she was driving." Chuck added.

"Oh, uh-oh," I replied, "I didn't think about that happening."

We all imagined, in our own version, Hilary opening her over-sized pocket book while driving down the curvy mountain road and the chipmunk jumping out, causing her to wreck her car.

Some of us looked worried, while some of us were smiling, none of us meant to give away our true thoughts, but facial expressions are always the real truth behind our words. Regardless of what anyone says, the face tells the truth.

Bo had a blank stare, I don't really think he had a clue what was going on.

"Well, I'm tired," I said, as I placed my empty beer bottle on the bar and started to walk away. Y'all have a good night and see you all at work tomorrow."

"If we still have jobs, tomorrow. We don't even know who the new boss is, yet." Chad added. "You never know, it could be bad for all of us."

"Well, we have to show up to work to get fired, so, either way, see you tomorrow." I replied, as I waved goodnight to everyone.

"Hey, man, I'll walk out with you." Chuck said as he followed me outside.

"You forgot Jenny." I said joking around - and just in case he really did forget her.

"Don't worry about that, she's hot. She'll find a ride back to the house." said Chuck as we walked through the parking lot.

"What? Are you messing with me? I'll give her a ride home!" I replied, jokingly.

'Yeah I bet, man!' he said as he shoved me. "No way, Abbott! I'm joking. She'd kill me if I did that. But no, let's be serious a minute..."

"What's up?"

"Chad has a point, in a way, about getting fired." he said as we walked to my car.

"What do you mean?" I asked.

"Word has it that the office manager, Amelia, is going to be the new GM. She's good friends with Hilary. I don't know if it's true, but I heard a couple of the Board Members talking about it at work while they were sitting in the lobby talking."

"Oh, no." I sighed, 'You have got to be kidding me, man."

"I'm not.' Chuck added. "If she is named the next general manager then everybody who Hilary hates, especially you, are going to have their jobs made as difficult as hell, until everyone quits or is fired once they can get enough proof that you, and others, are not doing their jobs properly."

I just thought about it and didn't know what to say.

"In other words -" Chuck began to say.

"I'm screwed." I finished the sentence.

"Yeah, you, me, about half of everybody that works there." he replied.

"Damn. I don't love the job, but it's a job and I need it a little longer until something better comes along." I said in despair.

"Don't say anything to anybody yet." he said. "I don't want everyone to panic but I thought I would let you know so if it does happen you have heads up on finding another job."

"What job?" I blurted. "I wouldn't work there if I didn't have to, but hell, it's the best of the worst jobs available, and that's all there is right now. Shitty jobs!"

"Well, just keep it in the back of your mind. None of us have done anything to cause us to get fired, but they will make life Hell until it's possible."

"Or quit first." I added.

"Yeah, but who can afford to quit?" asked Chuck, making a good point.

I shrugged and sat down in the driver's seat of my crappy blue hot rod.

"Damn," I added, "Bo, probably will be the first to go. He's already made plenty of mistakes."

"Yeah, that's a possibility.' Chuck replied. "Donald kept him around because he felt sorry for him. Regardless of who the new boss is, I doubt anyone else would do the same."

"I feel bad for him, more than I do for anybody else." I added as I shook my head and cranked my car.

"See you later, Abbott." Chuck said as he walked away.

"Yep, later." I replied.

I sat in my car and just stared off into nothing. Here I was, barely getting by as a security guard with a college degree, who should be a journalist and I'm about to get fired because the new, possible, boss is good friends with Hilary, and if she's friends with Hilary then she has to be a jealous mean ass bitch, too, or else they wouldn't be friends. 'Two of a feather flock together'. I didn't know Amelia, I had seen her several times, but she never smiled or spoke to me... then it hit me, yep she was probably just like Hilary.

Thank God tomorrow was payday. At least I had something to look forward to at work. Damn I was mad more than I was bummed out, because I finally had a job, no matter how crappy, with a great boss, and the fucker goes and dies on me; leaving us with the wicked witches of the mountain.

Although, then again, when one door closes, another one opens... which reminded me: Maybe Hilary did open her pocketbook while she was driving and plunged down the side of a mountain in a fiery crash - not to suffer - hopefully it killed her instantly. Normally, I would feel bad about that, like I had earlier, but not so much now. I would never intentionally hurt anyone, but maybe this was a gift from God. Speaking of God - I'm sure I was going to Hell for thinking that.

Oh, well... couldn't be any worse than working at Sugar Peak. Could it?

Nah, the more I thought about it, and the people I had met and the new co-worker friends that I had made, it wasn't that bad - Sugar Peak wasn't.

CHAPTER 15:

THE NIGHT THE CAR WENT DOWN THE SKI SLOPES

I was a little nervous when I arrived at work the next day and Hilary wasn't there. Nobody mentioned anything about a fiery crash down the side of a mountain, and I didn't ask.

Donald Spacey's office was locked and nobody was making any worthy decisions except for Chuck and the Maintenance Department Manager, Jerry.

"Did you hear what happened to Hilary?" Chad eagerly said, as he looked around to make sure no one else was listening, barely being able to contain his amusement.

"No." I said worried. "Is it bad?"

"Apparently she left her bag here after work by mistake, so nothing bad happened on her way home." he replied.

"Oh, thank God." I mumbled. "I was worried that I accidentally hurt or killed her! I mean, I don't care for her, but there's a big difference from not liking someone who's a bitch and wanting them hurt or killed. Thank God!"

"No, man. No! Wait, it gets better!" he added.

"Huh?"

"Yeah, listen to this!" Chad explained as I couldn't wait to hear what was so funny to him, hoping it was nothing bad. "When she got to work this morning she opened that over-sized ridiculous pocketbook that you put the chipmunk in, and it jumped out - or climbed out - whatever chipmunks do - and it scared the shit out of her! Apparently she freaked out and turned to run away and slammed right into the wall! It knocked her out and EMS had come take her away in an ambulance!"

"That's horrible." I said, in shock, yet feeling better nothing too bad happened.

"Yeah, that's horrible! That poor little chipmunk had to stay in there all night." he replied, "No telling what was in there with it. It could have died, but it didn't! Everything's fine!"

"At least she didn't wreck or anything like that." I replied.

"Yeah, they're just running CAT scans and M.R.I.'s to make sure she's okay. I think they're going to keep her overnight for observation, for precaution." Chad said with a smile.

"Well, that's good." I nodded.

"Yeah, but the chipmunk is running around here someplace." said Chad as his face turned serious. "I just hope we find it before one of our guests or members find it first."

"Well, if it ends up in Helen's condo we won't have to worry about it. She doesn't know what's going on most of the time anyways." I said thinking aloud.

"Who?"

"Never mind," I said, "it's a lady who seems to be past the point of no return. It's nothing."

"Oh, the old lady Jerry accidentally whacked with the broom? I heard about that." Chad said. "I wish I was there! That shit sounded hilarious."

"It was, actually." I replied, thinking about Jerry trying to beat the chipmunk with the broom.

"Thanks for that," I added, "I don't feel so bad for hiding the Chipmunk in Hilary's bag. It couldn't have been as bad as trying to get beat to death by a one-eyed, scary-looking, man with a broom handle."

"You're welcome." he replied.

I began walking to the elevator, and then it happened. I was expecting it, but not right at this moment. The words I didn't want to hear.

"Did you hear that Amelia is going to be our new boss?" Chad said. "It was made official a few hours ago."

"I'm sorry, what did you say?" I asked, wishing that I heard him incorrectly.

"Amelia is our new General Manager. It was made official a few hours ago by the board in a memo. "he replied. "I'm surprised that Chuck didn't get the job. He's way better with people and is more qualified. Everybody likes him. All the employees and members think he's awesome, but I guess they did what they thought was the right choice."

"Amelia is our new boss?" I asked. "And Chuck didn't get the job?"

"Yep." he replied.

"Are you sure?" I asked.

"Yeah." he replied, astonished I would ask three times, as if I was asking like it was a bad thing. It was a bad thing.

"Well, good for her." I said, keeping my thoughts to myself.

"She's at the hospital right now." said Chad. "She went to check on Hilary."

That was bad news. Nobody here would go to the hospital to check on Hilary. She was a bitch to everyone and would never go out of her way to help anyone else. She was manipulative to the members, mean to the employees and would stab you in the back the first chance she had. If Amelia was willing to go see her in the hospital then we were all going to get fired, probably. Especially me.

"She called about thirty minutes ago and said she wanted to talk to me when my shift is over. She said she'll be back in about an hour or so." Chad said with excitement. "I wonder if I'm getting promoted? That would be cool."

I immediately realized that it was already happening and Chad was the first victim of her inquisition.

"Hey," I asked, "quick question. Do you and Hilary get along?"

He laughed, "Heck no! I mean, we tolerate each other but we don't really like each other. I'm always cracking on her any chance I get. I can't help it! She's so mean to everybody so I just throw it back, but I smile and laugh in a friendly way. I don't say anything that crosses the line. Why?"

"Just wondering." I said as I walked away. I didn't want to worry about it the rest of his shift. Whether I was wrong or right it wouldn't help to tell him I knew he was going to get fired. Suddenly I hated this place more than I did the day I started, but for a different reason. I didn't hate this 'place' as much as I did the new management.

"See you after a while." I said as I stepped into the elevator and headed up to the top floor to do my security hall walking.

"Hey partner!" Scotty yelled from down the hall.

I waved. I wasn't in the mood to socialize.

"What the hell is wrong with you?" Scotty asked, as he stood in the hallway, leaning on his cane. "Looks like you just caught your wife giving a blowjob to your neighbor in the garage, or worse - someone just ran over your dog!"

"No," I replied. "Neither one of those."

"Well, I think I know," he said as he walked closer, "we all lost a good man a few days ago and it's been weighing heavy on all our hearts. I'm sure he was a great man to work for and everybody is really going to miss him."

"Yeah," I answered, "That's not the only person or thing I'm going to miss."

"What are you talking about, Abbott" he demanded, "What do you know that I don't?"

"Let's just put it this way," I said, "We lost Marcus Aurelius and inherited Commodus."

"You've lost me,' he said, "are those Roman emperors?"

"We traded President Roosevelt for Hitler and his SS Storm troopers."

"What the hell are you talking about? Just say it, Abbott. It's me you're talking to, not some goddamn tattletale!" he blurted, as I could see his concern for my worries. "No matter what you tell me about this place I'm not going to get you in trouble or repeat anything you say. I'm not one of these bastards that have nothing better to do than stir up trouble for people."

"I know," I mumbled, "I just felt like if I said it, they'd somehow find out and fire me earlier than planned. Are there microphones in these hallway surveillance cameras?"

"Who's going to fire you?" he asked, "Just a day or two before Donald passed away, he told me what a great job you were doing and they were happy to have you as an employee. That's a bunch of horse shit!"

"I don't know what to do." I replied.

"Come inside, we will talk in my condo." said Scotty as he motioned for me to follow him inside his place.

"Hilary," I said as I sighed and proceeded to explain the whole situation. I told him about how Hilary was such a bitch to everyone and how Amelia, the new boss, was very good friends with her. For their vengeance on everyone who made them jealous or who they just didn't like were getting fired so they could bring in their own demented, twisted, bitchy friends to take our jobs (probably) and that with Amelia in charge, and Hilary as her best friend, it was pretty much like we were all working for Hilary. I explained everything, even what I did with the chipmunk in her over-sized ugly pocket book.

"Well, that chipmunk thing is goddamn funny!" he replied, "but the rest of that shit pisses me off!"

"Well, I might not be here much longer, and if not, I just wanted to say it was a pleasure getting to know you and thanks for being friendly and nice to me. You've been a good friend, Scotty. Thank you." I said, trying to hold back my emotions.

"I've got an idea." he said, "it'll take a few days, maybe a week, but hang in there! Don't give them any reason to fire you, and do not tell anybody you put that chipmunk in her bag. If anyone else knows make sure that they swear they will not tell anyone! I promise you won't get fired for a few days, I'll make sure to that, but that's all I can promise for now."

"How are you going to do that?" I asked.

"Well, not that it's anybody's business," explained Scotty, "but I pledged a million dollars to this place as a gift in honor of my memory after I die, and I'll just tell them that if I find out anybody got fired without a good reason I'll take that away in a heartbeat."

"Thank you." I replied, "You can count on it. I'll do my best not to get fired for at least a few days - or a week."

"I hope so!" he added, "my god you're a damn college graduate who seems to have a good head on his shoulders. Don't let me down!"

"I won't, Scotty." I said.

"You sure as hell better not." he replied.

I left his condo and continued down the hall and finished my security rounds on and in the property.

By the end of the night I walked to the front desk to speak to Chad before I left for the night.

"If you're looking for Chad he's already left for the evening." a lady said as she came around the corner from the office and up to the front desk.

She had bad hair and a slight gap between her teeth. Her eyes vibrated as she stared at me with a look of hidden evil. I had only met here once before, briefly, but I soon remembered that this face of Satan was Amelia in the flesh.

I wasn't sure what to say. Should I ask if he was fired and raise suspicion against myself? Should I try to find out why and just ask why he left? I didn't know what to say. I was also worried she was going to fire me while she had me right in front of her in a quiet, large, and desolate lobby.

"Oh." Is all that I could get to come out of my pansy ass mouth.

"Is there anything I can help you with, uh, Security Abbott?" she said, reading my name tag.

I shook my head, wanting to think of something to say to find out if she fired him.

"Wait- so you're C.F. Abbott?" she asked.

"As far as I know I am." I replied, suddenly realizing that my smart mouth sometimes spoke at the wrong time. The last thing I needed was to smart-off to the new boss, already.

"I've got my eyes on you." she said, "I don't know if you'll work out here, but we'll see. Just know that I'm watching you."

"Okay, good stuff." I said.

"Are you going to be a problem?" she added, staring at me with devil eyes. "I just want you to know that if YOU had anything to do with the rodent in Hilary's bag - if you had anything to do with that little prank, I will break you until you run home crying for you mommy."

"Well," I replied, now feeling justified to smart-off, "my 'mommy' isn't here. As in, she's dead, so I seriously doubt that's possible, but I'll keep that in mind. Thank you. Oh, and one more thing, Scotty, you know the guy with the million dollar pledge wants to speak with you soon as possible. He asked me to tell you that."

He didn't ask me, but I was pissed that she brought my mom into this.

"Okay, thanks." she said, "Have a good night."

"You too." I said as I walked away.

"By the way," she added, "Chad was fired tonight. I won't tolerate employees berating and harassing other employees."

"Well, then, when Hilary comes back to work maybe you should fire her, too." I replied as I kept walking. It felt good to say.

"I've got my eyes on you and my ears open, Abbott!" she said loudly as to make sure I could hear her.

"Yes ma'am." I said, still walking away, with a smile.

I called Chad on my way home from work. I couldn't hear him because of the loud noise in the background. I don't know if he could hear me clearly, but I did hear him say "Figgie's." It was a bar with a live band every night.

Figgie's was clear across the mountain and it had started to snow. If I was smart I would have gone straight home, but I wasn't so I decided to meet Chad there to make sure my friend was okay after being fired from his job.

When I arrived at the bar it had started snowing pretty heavy, but this was November in the mountains and was normal to start getting heavy snowfall beginning around this time of the year.

"Abbott!" he slurred from across the bar. "I've already made out with one girl and another one was dancing with me and put her hand down my pants and squeezed my junk. I'm having an awesome time, dude!"

I glanced down to see what Chad was doing with his hand, which was currently down his own pants.

"Is she playing with your junk right now?" I asked.

"Huh? Oh." he muttered as he quickly pulled his hand out of his pants and turned red from embarrassment.

"I hope nobody noticed me doing that to myself!" he blurted.

"I wouldn't worry about that bro.' I replied, "I don't think most people in here can see much of anything clearly, at the moment."

"Good," he said, "me neither!"

"Let's get you home, man." I said, knowing we needed to leave before the roads became impassable. "I'll drive."

"Why man? No!" he said, "I'm not finished drankin' my beer."

"You can 'drank' your beer in the car." I replied, "Come on buddy, let's go. It's snowing and the roads are getting bad. If you wait any longer you'll be stuck way over here without a place to stay."

"Well," he added as he took a gulp of his beer and it poured from the sides of his mouth, "let me say goodbye to that girl I was making-out with a few minutes ago. I'm not leaving until I do!"

"Okay, I replied, "Which one is she."

"She's the brunette in the green shirt. Where ever she is." he answered.

I scanned the room and then I noticed a brunette in a green shirt as she walked close by us and on across the room. She was hideous.

"Trust me, you're better off letting that one go." I said as I grabbed him by the arm and we walked out.

"Okay! That bad, huh? She looked hot to me, but I'm a little drunk!" he whispered loudly.

I drove my car quickly, but carefully, because I wanted to get further down the road before the weather became worse.

"Hey, it's snowing, man!" he exclaimed as he looked at the snowflakes falling outside in the headlights of my car.

"Yeah, sure is buddy." I said as we continued driving across the dangerous mountain road, "Who knew it was going to snow? Nobody. I think I have the skill and scientific knowledge to be a meteorologist - weatherman. All I need is coin to flip and somebody to listen as if what I say matters. - There's a fifty percent chance I'm full of shit and it might snow, or rain, whatever. I'll have all the details after something happens... stay tuned!"

"You sound like a professional dude!" Chad said, laughing and gagging at the same time. "My grandmother always said that the first big snow of the season was a sign of new beginnings and fresh starts. I guess in a way this is my 'new beginning'." he slurred.

"Amelia fired you, didn't she?" I said quietly, as I put a cigarette in my mouth and handed one to him.

I lit mine, then gave him the lighter. He took a few drags off of his cigarette before saying a word. "Yeah, she did."

"I'm sorry, man." I said, "that's not right. She did you wrong. We're going to fix that, if we can."

"How?" he asked.

"Well," I shrugged, "I can't really say anything right now, but Scotty is going to help us."

"Scotty, who lives in the building?" he asked.

"The only Scotty I know." I replied.

"When did you talk to him?" he asked, "How did you find out so quickly?"

"Well, rumors were swirling around that Amelia was going to be GM a couple of days ago." I explained. "Apparently she and Hilary are the best of friends. Hilary, who hates us all, is the driving force behind all this."

"Who told you all this?" he asked, frantically.

"Well, it's not just rumors anymore, it's proven to be the truth now. Obviously." I said.

"Why did you hear about this and I didn't? he asked. "Why didn't you tell me? How come you didn't say anything?"

"I didn't know you, specifically, were going to get fired, not this quick." I explained.

"Not this quick? Not this quick? What the hell does that mean? If you knew something you should have told me!" he blurted.

"Hey!" I snapped back, "I'm in the same boat you are! I'm just waiting my turn. Finding out a day in advance doesn't help you or any of us find a job any faster, it just ads stress knowing that it's going to happen!"

"Yeah, I guess you're right man." he replied. "I'm sorry."

"Don't worry about it." I mumbled through clinched teeth, holding my cigarette, "No reason to apologize. Just wait until I get fired. I'm going to be meaner and drunker than you."

"I guess the worst part is, you know about it and can't do anything about it." he said somberly.

"Like I said, there's a plan. I just have to hope I don't get fired for a few days so we can make it happen." I added.

"Can't wait to see what it is," he replied. "If it's anything like you did in college then I'm sure it's going to be good!"

"Honestly, I have no idea what the plan is." I said.

"That makes no sense." he said.

I looked at him, although in a slight drunken stupor he made perfect sense. "Trust me." I replied.

"Okay," he said drunkenly, "I'll trust you. This is weird."

"What is?"

"This, right now," he replied, "because were here, in your car and I had a dream that I was in your car and we were driving somewhere and it was snowing! That's crazy!"

"Chad, you're drunk. That was probably just your memory from a few minutes ago." I said, trying not to laugh. I felt bad that he had lost his job today for no good reason except that certain people were on an inquisition.

"I had a crazy dream the other night." I added.

"What did you dream, dude?" he asked.

"I had a dream - I think it was a dream - that I was mooning cars out on the street, in honor of the 40th anniversary of the moon landing. I was saying something like: 'That's one small ass for man, one giant of an asshole for mankind'. I'm pretty sure it was a dream because I was wearing a spacesuit... but then again, I did wake up that morning wearing a white shirt, white boxers and a football helmet. Actually, I'm not sure. I hope it was a dream-"

"Watch out!" he yelled as he pointed.

I quickly looked to see a deer standing in the middle of the snow-covered road. I instinctively hit the brakes and swerved to miss the deer.

Suddenly I lost control and we spun around and bounced down an embankment. (Remember we had traveled across a mountain road, near the top of a pass, because the bar was across the other side of Sugar) For some reason it felt like it was a long time, as my car barely missed a few trees and came to a stop at the edge of what seemed like a small cliff. At the moment I wasn't sure because my headlights had busted during our slide down the embankment.

"I just shit myself." Chad said.

"I think were okay, now." I spoke, too soon.

Suddenly, the car tilted forward and there was enough light to see where we were. The top of the ski slope had been very icy from the reports we had been given at work. I don't know why I hit the gas... maybe out of fright, panic or for whatever reason, I put it in reverse as we tiled forward. Luckily the so-called 'cliff' was only 3 or 4 feet high. We hit the icy ski slope and suddenly spun around. We began to slide backwards down the steep ski slope. The fresh-fallen snow wasn't deep enough to stop us from sliding.

We screamed, I think. We continued to slide down the ski slope until we came to a stop halfway down the bottom.

"I just shit myself." Chad said, again.

"I heard you the first time!" I replied, still grasping the steering wheel with a look of terror on my face.

"No," he replied, "I thought that was it, but it wasn't. I shit myself, again."

"It's okay." I think I replied, or something like that, still frozen in shock.

In a moment I smelled it.

"Oh, that smells. Bad." I said.

"Like shit!" Chad added, "Because I shit in my pants!"

"Right." I nodded, looking out of the windshield as if I was still driving.

"Where are we?" he asked.

"On the ski slopes." I answered.

"You're shittin' me!" he replied.

I looked down in my lap. "No, I don't think I did, but I don't blame you for doing it."

"Thanks man." he said, uncomfortably. "So, - what do we do now?"

"We leave the car here and call it in stolen." I said.

"You think that will work?" he asked.

"It did last time." I replied.

"Last time?"

"Yeah, I did this once before, back in college with Mack, Ducky and Carp." I explained.

"Really?"

"Really."

"I'm beginning to think that you are not a very good driver." he said quietly.

"Nobody is a good driver when they're sliding down a ski slope!" I replied in my defense.

"Well, let's start walking." I said as we got out of my crappy old blue car.

"This sucks." Chad said.

"Yeah," I replied, "imagine having to walk home twice in one month."

"Huh?"

"Never mind, it's a long story." I said as we started walking down the mountain, very carefully.

CHAPTER 16:

THE POLICE FIND MY CAR, RIGHT WHERE I LEFT IT... ON THE SKI SLOPES

My phone vibrated on the nightstand next to my bed.

"Hello?" I answered half-asleep.

"Mr. Abbott?" the voice said.

"Yeah, who's this?" I asked.

"This is Officer Max Bell with the Sugar Mountain Police Department.

"Max? Max! Hey, man, it's me, Abbott; Chuck's friend."

"Abbott! Hey, I didn't really put two and two together." he said, with a more friendly tone.

"What's up, Max? How have you been?"

"Good! I'm good. Didn't lose my job after all!" he said.

"Well, that's good news." I replied, not knowing what to say.

"Hey, Abbott, I was calling to tell you that we found your car." he said.

"Really? Oh, that's great, Max. Uh, thanks."

There was a moment of silence...

"Don't you want to know where we found it?" he asked.

"Oh, yeah. Yeah! Absolutely. So, where did you find it?" I asked.

"On the ski slopes." he said bluntly.

"Really?" I replied, trying to sound astonished.

"Don't you want to ask if we arrested the person who stole it?" he said.

"You arrested someone?" I asked, confused.

"No, we didn't arrest anyone because it was abandoned as if someone accidentally drove off the road and slid down the ski slope."

"Wow," I added, "that sounds like it must have been... terrifying."

"It must have been because we found a stool in your car." he said.

"A stool?" I asked, "Like a bar stool? I don't remember that..."

"What was that?" he asked, "I'm sorry, you were mumbling a little."

"Nothing, nothing." I said. "What kind of 'stool'?"

"A bowel movement kind of stool, Abbott." he explained.

"That's horrible." I replied, as I had momentarily forgotten about that.

"Guess what else we found in your car." he said.

I thought about it for a moment.

"I give up. What?"

"We found your car keys, Abbott!" he said loudly. "Why would your cars keys be in the car?"

I was busted, he knew it.

"You mean somebody stole my keys? What a bastard!"

"Oh, cut the crap, Abbott!" he blurted.

"I'm not cutting or touching any crap," I replied, 'that's nasty."

"I bet it was nasty," he said, "who's is it?"

"How - how would I know? I reported my car stolen, remember?" I said.

"Yeah, sure."

"Which reminds me -" I started to say.

"Don't even go there Abbott!" he said quietly, "we agreed to keep that to ourselves. I'm lucky to still have my job because of you!"

"Me?"

"Yes, you!"

"It was your idea-"

"Just forget it! Please." he whispered.

"Speaking of jobs - I have to get to mine today, so can I pick it up." I asked.

"No, you can't drive it." he said, "It's not going anywhere."

"Why?"

"Because it took a beating when you drove it off the road and went down the ski slope!"

"Oh, I don't - know anything about that." I said.

"Whatever." he replied.

"Hey, can I get a ride to work, maybe?" I asked.

"Well," he stated, "I would give you a ride but I don't have a patrol car!"

"Oh. Yeah. Sorry about that." I said.

"But I'll send someone to pick you up so you can have your car towed to wherever you want to fix it." Max replied.

"Thank you."

"Someone will be there in twenty minutes. Be ready." he demanded.

"No problem. Thanks. Max." I said.

"You owe me." he replied.

"Doesn't this make us even?" I asked.

"No." he said, "No it does not."

"Alright-" I agreed, as he hung up on me.

I got out of bed and tried to find a clean shirt. I noticed a slight hint of an unpleasant smell.

"Maybe a shower first." I told myself.

The whole day at work I never saw Amelia one time. My shift passed slowly without incident. I did everything perfectly, exactly like my duties as a security officer were supposed to be completed. I walked around, smiled at people and kept a vigilant eye out for any trouble. It was boring. I hardly spoke to anyone. It felt strange, but so far, so good. I still had my job.

CHAPTER 17:

ENCOURAGING WORDS FROM MY WACKY OLD DAD

I drove down to my hometown to visit my dad in the nursing home.

I waited, as usual, at the locked door that connected his hall to the rest of the nursing home. In a moment an employee opened the door for me.

When I arrived to his room I found him sitting in his wheelchair eating crackers and watching TV. There was only one problem: he didn't have any pants on and had his shirt tucked into his underwear.

"Hey, pops," I said, "hoping today was good day, "how is - everything?"

"Well, hello boy!" he replied with a grin, "How've you been?"

"I'm good." I answered as I sat down in a chair next to him.

I wasn't sure whether to say anything or not. I didn't want to upset him.

"I got a roommate." he said as he munched down on a cracker.

"A roommate?" I replied.

"Yeah, what did you think the other bed was for, company?" he stated, as he took a sip of his glass of milk and shook his head.

I shrugged.

"His name is Walter, and he's bonkers. That son-of-a-bitch

doesn't know purple from Tuesday." Dad said as he kept talking through a mouth full of crackers and milk, "He stole my belt the other day and wouldn't give it back. Every time I ask him about it he takes off running down the hall like a chicken set on fire. Damn crazy fool."

"Speaking of which," I added, "uh, where are your pants?"

"He stole my pants too!"

"Well, pops, you have more than one pair." I replied.

"I don't want to wear my other ones." he blurted, "my jeans are uncomfortable, my other slacks are too stiff and I'm not walking around all day in my pajama pants. Do you know how unprofessional that looks?"

"Pop, you're in a nursing home, I don't think anyone will care-"

"Well, I care!" he interrupted, "Some of these ladies, no matter how crazy I am, think that I'm the best thing since dentures. The men in here want to be me and the women want to be with me. I have a standard and a persona to uphold. It's true."

"Okay, pops." I said, "Well, at the moment you have your flannel shirt tucked into your tighty-whities. Is that part of your persona?"

He looked down in his lap, "Ah, hell, hand me my pajamas out of that top drawer, will you."

I grabbed his pajama pants and helped him put them on.

"So, pops, I have a question." I said as I continued to help him put on his pajamas while he wiggled around to help him in his wheelchair.

"No, I do not have any illegitimate children - that I know of!" he chuckled.

"That's good to know." I replied, as I sat back down in the chair next to him. "What would you do if a boss that you liked died and a real bad person took his place and started firing everyone because he, or she, didn't want anyone who could be a threat to their job one day from working there any longer?"

"Well, first of all," he said, "I don't know how a person like that got the job in the first place, probably from lying and being manipulative, but secondly, if I could I would go talk to the powers-to-be. There's always somebody higher up than the boss. Find out who that is and talk to them."

"What if the real power players are the ones who made this person the boss?" I asked.

"Then either explain the situation or quit before you get fired, if you haven't been already. You don't need that on your work record." he said.

"What makes you think that I'm going to get fired?" I asked. Wondering if he still thought I was a screw-up.

"Because you're a leader son, in everything you've done and will do. People flock to you." he explained as I listened carefully, "They trust you. I've seen it your whole life. Even when you were doing something you shouldn't as a kid, you were always the leader who talked other kids into getting in trouble with you. Why? Because they looked up to you and trusted you. Whatever is going on now, son, I know you will do the right thing."

"Even if the right thing involves causing someone else to lose their job, no matter if they're a person with a bad attitude, but not necessarily a bad-bad person?" I asked.

"You have to make that judgment call own your own, Charlie." he replied, "A person with a bad attitude, no matter how good they are as the law is concerned, is still a bad person to have to deal with at work, especially if they're a liar and manipulative."

I nodded as I thought about what he had told me.

"Son, life is going to be filled with obstacles," he added, "you of all people should know how difficult life can be. You're a living example of detours, heart-breaks, injuries, betrayals and prejudice. Learn from your experiences, use the brain God gave you and keep on truckin'."

"Thanks pops" I said as I gave him a kiss on his head. "I needed to hear that from you."

"You're welcome." he replied, "Now do me a favor."

"What would that be?"

"Get my damn pants back from Walter!" he demanded, "You can't miss him. He's the old weirdo chasing imaginary cats down the hallway."

"No promises, pops." I replied.

"Old crazy fools." he added, 'everybody in this place is loony."

"Except you." I said.

"Except me!" he said.

"I love you Dad. I'll see you next time." I said as I walked out of his room.

"With my pants on!" he yelled.

"With your pants on." I agreed.

CHAPTER 18:

TELL 'EM 'MIKE HUNT' IS HERE… & BO HAS AN ACCIDENT

I arrived at the first gate at work. It didn't open. A security guard whom I had not seen before stepped out of the gatehouse and walked over to my vehicle.

"Is there something I can help you with?" he asked.

I was in my security uniform and had driven through this gate almost every day for over a month. I thought it would be obvious.

"I work here." I answered.

"Where's your employee sticker that goes in the front right corner of your windshield?"

"I never got one." I replied, "This is a rental car."

"Name?" he asked.

"Who are you? We haven't met." I said with a fake smile.

"Name?" he asked, again. He wasn't friendly.

"Mike." I replied, "Mike Hunt."

"Okay, give me a minute," he said, "Since you don't have a pass I'll have to call and check it out."

"Okay." I replied.

A few minutes later.

"I'm sorry but we have no records that saying that Mike Hunt works here."

"Oh, what about C.F. Abbott?" I asked, showing him my driver's license.

He stood there for a moment as it all sunk in. He then realized what he had said when he called the main office.

"C.F. Abbott?" he replied, becoming a little embarrassed and mad at the same time. "Yeah, I've heard of you. I have a note here that says Amelia wants to speak with you when you arrive."

"Uh-huh." I replied. I soon thought that maybe this was the day I was fired. I don't know why I cared so much, but I did. I wasn't sure if Scotty was able to do whatever it was he was going to do, but my stomach felt as if it had lifted into my chest and I began to feel slightly nauseated.

"You can go." he said as the gate arm raised.

"Where's Bo? He usually works today, right?" I asked.

"I don't know anything about that." he replied. "Have a nice day."

I left the asshole behind in my dust as I gunned the little electric car. I sped away in what sounded like a golf cart. I drove on up to the Peak and through the second gate and parked around back, in the owner's lot. I figured that if I was going to get fired it didn't really matter where I parked, and besides, I wasn't in my crappy blue car, I had a rental.

I took my time walking in the building and clocking in, partly because a gust of wind blew my hat off my head and I had to chase it across the parking lot - and then because I wasn't in a hurry to get fired.

I walked into the security office where Security Steve, the chief, was sitting at his desk doing paper work.

"Hi, Security Abbott. How are you today?" he said in his usual nerdy, stuttered voice.

"So far, so good. I think." I replied.

"I have a special assignment for you today," he said as he stood up with a sheet of paper in his hand and walked around his desk to hand it to me.

"What's that?" I asked.

"It's very important!" he said with a big grin.

"Okay..."

"I need you to fill out your insurance information" he explained, thinking it was a funny joke the way he had said it. "This will be for your health insurance that the resort provides for its employees. Congratulations, you made it past the forty-five-day probationary period.

"Don't count your security officers before they hatch." I mumbled as I let the paper fall out of my hand and it landed on his desk. I walked out and down the hall towards the main lobby.

I was ready to get this bullshit finished. I was going to confront Amelia face-to-face and let her go ahead and fire me. I noticed Hilary was back at work as she gave me a glare and a smirk, like a fat little girl in elementary school would do as I walked into the principal's office.

"Oh, I'm fine, thanks for asking." she remarked sarcastically.

"Glad to hear." I replied, "Those chipmunks can really be a pain in the ass, huh – and those walls, too, I hear."

I smiled on the inside.

I walked down the short hall to the general manager's office. It reminded me of the first time I had been here when I was interviewed by Donald Spacey for the job. The weird part was: The first time I walked into that office I did it against my will, grudgingly accepting that I need this job. Now, I walked down this hall on my own, not because I had to, but because I wanted to, except this time, against my will I was about to grudgingly accept that I was getting fired.

"C.F., have a seat." Amelia said as she stood behind her desk.

I at least tried to be polite and wait for her to sit down first. She waited on me. I started to sit down and then I stopped, she did the same. Both of us were waiting for the other to sit down first and it became awkwardly funny - to me.

"Sit down!" she demanded.

I sat down.

"How can I be of service." I said, slightly joking.

"C.F., do you enjoy working here?" she asked, as she tapped a pen in her right hand and adjusted her glasses for the big move of setting me up to say yes and then dropping the fire-bomb on me.

"Uh, call me Abbott, not C.F., and no." I replied.

"No, what?" she asked, confused.

"No, I do not like working here. The pay sucks, the king is dead and now we are all ruled by the queen with the poisonous apple."

"I'm sorry, are you being a smart ass?" she asked.

Now I was slightly confused, "What? No, you asked me if I like working here and I answered honestly."

"Well... at least your honest." she said as she picked up my file and started looking over it. "It says here that you have a B.A. degree in History."

"I prefer to call it a B.S. degree, and it's in Communications." I replied.

"It says B.A. right here." she said, not understanding my joke.

"That's correct." I said in a serious tone.

"Then, you went to movie school?" she asked.

"Journalism School." I corrected her. "What's the difference; does it matter?" she asked.

"It doesn't matter here!" I replied with a smile.

"Let me ask you something, C.F.-"

"Abbott, call me Abbott" I corrected her, again.

"C.F.," she said, letting me know she wasn't going to listen to me. "Where do you see yourself in five years? Do you hope to make a career out of your job here at the resort?"

"No." I said bluntly with a smile. "No, a career is something you study first so that you can make a good living doing something professional. This, on the other had is a job. I don't really hate my job, but I don't like it neither. I did for a brief moment, but that moment passed and now I stay up late applying for jobs online and put my current job on my applications as 'The Gatekeeper of Hell'."

"Why do you do that?" she asked.

"Do what?"

"Do that! Why do you make everything I ask you into a dramatic answer with Shakespearean dialect?"

I had no clue what she was talking about. I just looked at her and smiled. I had no idea how to answer that question.

"Shakespeare?" I asked.

"Don't patronize me, C.F., I have an associate's degree in business. You're not the only smart brain around here!" she said as she closed my file folder and dropped it on her desk. "You've already wasted enough of my time, so let me get to the point. Scotty has made it clear to me that you are one of his favorite employees and that he goes fishing with a couple of the Board Members. Apparently, and I don't know where he got this from, he thinks I am firing people on a power trip and that if I happen to fire you without a good reason that he will not only withdraw his promise of a million dollar pledge to our resort but he will also complain about me until the Board of Director's fire me. So, therefore, I want you to know that you're not getting fired, for now, but I promise I will make your job a living hell until you quit!"

A moment of silence.

"I already told you I don't like my job," I replied, "I don't plan on being here in five years and I have no dreams to use my education to rise through the ranks to be a threat to your job. I am not your competition, Amelia; I am just a guy who has a job that pays the bills until something better comes along."

"Good." she said.

"But," I continued, "I do like the people here, except for you and your master. I have learned a lot since I started here and made some good friends. You fired Chad for a dumb reason. If anybody should be fired it's Hilary. Oh, and you had no right firing Bo. He doesn't have many skills, but he means well. He wasn't a threat to anybody but himself."

I started to walk out of her office.

"I didn't fire, Bo." she said firmly, "He was in a car accident on his way to work. He's alive. He should be okay, but he was hurt pretty bad. That's all we know so far." I could tell as she looked down at her desk and her voice trailed off that she might actually have a shred of decency for other humans after all.

"Where is he?" I asked, very worried. "What happened?"

"I don't know much more than just what I told you. Hopefully we'll get an update soon." she replied, and then followed by saying. "Abbott, don't leave before your shift is over, or else I'll have to fire you for leaving your job without permission!"

"You just called me Abbott." I replied.

"Don't even think about it!" she demanded.

"Well, if someone can get fired for leaving work to see a co-worker who is in the hospital because of a near-death car accident then I guess I'm fired." I replied as I hurried away to go see Bo at the hospital.

When I arrived at the hospital it started to snow.

"I'm looking for -" suddenly I realized that I had never learned Bo's last name. "Bo."

"What's the patient's last name?" the lady at the information desk asked.

"Bo... I don't know." I replied.

"Well, I'm sorry, young man, but I can't help you unless you know his last name." she said.

"He came in today. He was in a car accident. Can you look it up that way?" I asked.

"Let's see..." she began to search her system. "Wait, we have a Robert Francis who was just admitted to ICU. I don't know if-"

"Thank you very much!" I said as I ran toward the elevator.

ICU was on the 3rd floor.

At the nurses desk I asked for Robert Francis and they pointed down the hall.

"Last room on the left." said the nurse.

The door was cracked open. It was very quiet and poorly lit in the room as I opened the door.

"Can I help you?" said a young woman.

"That sounds familiar," I replied, "I think I'm in the right room. Bo?"

She nodded and looked over at the hospital bed.

What I saw was not what I expected. I wasn't really sure what I was going to expect, but it bothered me to see him in the hospital bed with a tube down his throat and both his arms in casts and a bandage on his head.

"I'm Melissa, Bo's wife." she said, shaking my hand.

I gave her a hug. I felt it was more needed than a handshake. "I'm Abbott." I said, "I work with your husband."

"Oh! Abbott. Bo talks about you all the time!" she replied, "Well, it is so nice to finally meet you."

"He does?" I asked, surprised.

"Yes, maybe too much." she smiled, "he really likes you and says how everybody looks up to you and how much fun you are to be around."

"Really?" I wondered how. I didn't see it. Suddenly what my father had told me a few days ago came rushing back into my mind and I realized that even in his condition he was still able to see the good things, and he held his memories of me close in his heart and struggled to hold them in his mind. He might not always remember that my mother was dead but the fact that he could tell me so much about myself that I never noticed meant very much to me.

"Yes." she tried to continue smiling as she carefully sat on the edge of the bed with her husband.

"If you don't mind me asking, what happened?" I asked.

"Well," she worked up the strength to relive the accident, "he called me while he was out running errands before he went to work. He called and said he didn't have time to go to pick up a paint sample from the hardware store because he didn't want to be late for work. He was telling me how worried he was that he was going to get fired because the new boss was really strict and mean. - The next thing I knew it sounded like a loud noise and as if he had dropped the phone. I heard him yelling and moaning so I hung up and called 911."

"I'm sorry." I said quietly.

"It's that new boss' fault!" she cried, "I hate her! I hate her so much right now."

I gave her another hug as I looked over her shoulder at Bo laying in the bed. I started to feel sick on my stomach. I felt really bad for him and Melissa.

"Don't worry about her," I said, "were going to fix this. I'm going to make this right. I promise."

She smiled and nodded as she wiped away her tears.

"Tell Bo I was here, please." I said as I took one more glance at him. "I have to get back to work, but tell him that I am thinking about him and I'll make it up to him.

"It's not your fault," she replied, "you don't have to make up for anything."

"I have a lot to make up for myself," I said somberly, "and if doing it for my friends is the way I can make it up to myself then that's what I'm going to do."

My phone rang as I was leaving the hospital. I didn't recognize the number.

"Hello?"

"Hey partner! You hanging in there!" Scotty yelled into the phone.

"Yeah, I'm still employed, thanks to you." I replied, "if not then I'm pretty sure she would have fired me an hour ago."

"Are you at work now?" he asked.

"No, I'm on my way back, though. I went to the hospital to see Bo, who works at the gatehouse. He was in an accident on his way to work today. He didn't want to be late or else Amelia was going to fire him."

"Are you serious?" he asked.

"I'm very serious, Scotty." I replied.

"Oh, no."

"Yeah, he looks pretty bad." I added.

"Well damn, you be careful! It's snowing. We don't need two good boys in the hospital!" he replied.

"Will do."

"Come see me when you get back up here! Alright?" he stated.

"Sure thing, Scotty. Gotta go. See you soon."

When I returned to work the gatehouse security officer let me up without stopping me this time. I'm sure he didn't want to have to talk to me, again.

I had to walk by the front desk to get to the elevators to go up to Scotty's condo.

"Well, there you are," Hilary snapped, "Mr. O'Neal needed someone to help him unload his car. I told him that you were probably sleeping or hiding out somewhere. He's on the Board of Director's and he's not too happy with you right now. He had to unload his car by himself.

"What do I look like? A fucking Bell Boy?" I replied, "There are two other security officers and five maintenance workers here at the moment. You could have asked anyone of them."

"Yes, but I couldn't have gotten them in trouble." she said with a smirk.

"Do I look like I care about this job?" I replied, "Do you really think I care if I'm in trouble, or not?"

She didn't say anything. People like her fed their evil, devious and jealous moods off of people's nerves, insecurities and the ability to make other people squirm. It didn't work on me.

I stepped off the elevator on the 10th floor. When I knocked on Scotty's door I already knew what was going to come out of my mouth before I said it.

"I care about this job!" I blurted. "I... I don't know why - maybe it's the good people or the evil bitches that need to be put in their place, but for some reason, whatever it is, I actually care about this job!"

"That's good." Scotty replied, "Better than hating the son-of-a-bitch, isn't it!"

"Well," I shrugged and nodded, "yeah. Absolutely."

"Are you ready to hear what we're going to do?" he asked as I walked into his condo.

"I don't think I could wait one minute longer." I replied. "I'm serious, in another minute I could get fired. You never know. So, literally, I can't wait another minute."

"Well, don't worry about that, anymore." he said as we walked into his living room. "I mean, don't do anything stupid and really get fired, but if you get fired for just doing your job don't sweat it. You'll only be unemployed for about a month, but it'll be worth it in the end."

"What exactly do you have up your sleeve, Scotty?" I asked, very curiously.

"Well, there's a board meeting this Saturday..." Scotty went on to explain to me his plan. I couldn't believe how generous and clever he was. I couldn't wait until Saturday at the Board of Director's Meeting.

CHAPTER 19:

SHE KNOCKED AND I WAS SHOCKED

It was late in the morning when I was making coffee with my new coffee maker. I heard a light knock at the door. I waited quietly to hear if it was Crazy Guy outside, but all I heard was another polite knock at my door.

I quickly opened the door and suddenly my eyes fell upon the most beautiful thing that God has ever created. You don't believe in God? Well, I might have been a little shaken on my belief until I gazed into the eyes of the most beautiful woman ever created. Only God could have created something this beautiful and she was living proof that there was a higher power.

I just froze in a serenity of good feelings as she looked into my own eyes and then smiled. I was instantly in love and I didn't know her name.

She seemed as stunned as I was, although to this day I don't know why. She was looking at me, but I was looking at her, the most beautiful creature, ever.

"Hi." she said, smiling.

"Hey." I said softly.

Suddenly I realized that love could actually knock on your door.

"I'm Abbott." I somehow managed to say.

"I'm Sophia." she replied.

"Hey faggot!" I heard a loud familiar voice say. I suddenly lost my connection for a moment.

"Jake!?" I said, surprised to see him at my door.

"Abbott!" he said as he grabbed me and slapped me on the back.

"What are you doing here?" I asked, still distracted by the beautiful blonde standing next to him.

"Hey, I want you to meet Sophia, my fiancée!" he said, as I felt as if I had just slammed into a brick wall.

"I've heard so much about you." she said, "it's nice to finally meet you."

"Yeah, nice to finally meet you too." I replied, very disappointed.

"Well, aren't you gonna invite us in?" he said with a big smile.

"Oh, yeah. Sure!" I replied as I backed away from the door so they could walk in my apartment.

Jake looked around the apartment with a confused look on his face. "Your place looks different than last time. What happened?"

"I cleaned it." I replied, to the fact.

"Oh. Yeah, it looks good, fucker!" he replied.

"Thanks." I said as I walked into the living room and we sat down on my couch.

"What are y'all doing here?" I asked, not having expected them, yet. Especially not someone as beautiful as her knocking on my front door.

I tried not to be rude, but I couldn't keep my eyes off of her.

"So how did you two lovebirds meet?" I asked.

"Through friends and family." she replied. I saw her looking at me too, and not just in a way of studying Jake's friends, but as if I knew that she too felt something when we first looked into each other's eyes. Hopeful and crazy? Maybe I was, but I had never had this strange feeling come over me so quickly about someone I had only met less than a second ago. It was magical and strange. It felt like a dream - as if she was the girl of my dreams. Nobody in their right mind believes in love at first sight, until it actually happens to them.

I believed from that moment onwards.

"We were passing through," Jake replied, "and I told her that we can't keep going without stopping in to see this shit for brains!"

"Yeah," I said, "that's me... Shit for brains!" I added, trying to smile and laugh while not letting my heartbreak be so obvious.

"How long are you staying?" I asked, feeling conflicted between not wanting them to stay and not wanting her beautiful face ever leaving my eyes.

"Just passing through." Jake replied. "We're going to have to leave in just a few minutes."

"I hate to hear that." I replied, honestly. I tried to look at him while he was talking, but I couldn't help but constantly glancing at her. She was the most beautiful thing God had ever created.

"So, what have you been up to lately, Abbott?" he asked.

"Yes," she added, "tell me who 'Abbott' is. Are you really like everything Jake has told me?"

"It depends on what he said." I answered joking around, "but whatever you heard, it's probably true."

She laughed while Jake nodded his head. There's no telling what he said about me, but I didn't care. I was - happy.

Suddenly sitting there with an old friend that I was afraid of, and a girl whom I had just met that I was instantly in love with, and a crappy job at a resort on top of a mountain, I realized that I was happy.

I looked at the time and it was almost 12 noon. "I have to get ready for work, but y'all can hang out here if you want for a little longer while I'm getting ready.

"No, we better go." Jake said as he stood up and Sophia did the same.

"Thanks for stopping by" I said as I looked into her eyes, "you have made my whole year."

She smiled, "It was very nice to meet you, Abbott. I hope we can see you again soon."

"Absolutely!" I replied as I snapped out of my gaze and looked at Jake and shook his hand.

"To hell with the hand-shaking!" he yelled as he grabbed me around the neck and gave me an uncomfortable hug that hurt.

"Thanks, man." I said, appreciating the visit and friendly attitudes from a beautiful fresh face and an old friend.

I gave Sophia a hug, too. When she gently put her arms around me it felt as if God had come down to earth and reached out and touched me.

"You two lovebirds be safe driving home!" I said as they walked outside.

"Don't worry about us!" Jake yelled back.

I watched as they walked away.

"Turn around. Turn around. Turn around." I said softly to myself, waiting for Sophia to turn and look at me one last time.

She did. She looked over her shoulder and smiled.

Suddenly I realized I was in love with Jake's fiancée and I felt bad about it. I closed the door and leaned up against it. I was happy for Jake. I was sad that I hadn't met her before he did. Why? I didn't know yet at the time, but later I realized that if it hadn't had been for Jake, I would have never met Sophia.

"I need a drink after that!" I said to myself as I reached in the cabinet to get the rum and a glass.

I started to pour my rum and mix it with a soft drink when I suddenly stopped. I didn't want to have a drink. It didn't entice me. I poured it out in the sink and walked to the bathroom to get ready for work.

CHAPTER 20:

NO GOOD DEED GOES UNPUNISHED

I was on my way out the door to go to work when I received a phone call.

"Hello?"

"Is this C.F. Abbott?" a man's voice asked.

"It depends on who is calling." I replied, wondering if I owed anyone money.

"This is Michael Janowski. I am Scotty and Christine Swift's attorney." he said.

"Oh, okay, good!" I replied, "he said I would hear from you soon!"

"Yes, but I am kind of calling for a different reason - in a way." he explained, "we've had to change our plan slightly..." his voice trailed off as if he was trying to figure out what to say to me.

"What do you mean? Everything is alright, I hope." I said enthusiastically.

"I'm sorry to have to be the one to tell you this, but Christine asked me to go ahead and call you. I don't know how to say this, but Scotty passed away last night. He went peacefully. He just went to sleep and never woke up." he said calmly.

I felt a sudden burst of weakness and shock as my stomach

churned and my eyes watered.

"Are you there, Mr. Abbott? Can you hear me?" he asked.

"Yeah - Yes, I'm here." I mumbled. I felt a great sadness come over my body.

"I'm very sorry for your loss, I know he put a lot of faith into you and only though you were in his life but for a short time I know he considered you a trusted friend or else he wouldn't have done what he did." Mr. Janowski said politely.

"What did he do? I'm sorry, I - I'm a little upset right now." I mumbled.

"Scotty made you the Chairman of his executive investment group that just bought a controlling stake in the resort where you worked and he lived. You will chair the company with supervision from myself and Scotty's widow."

"I do - what, now?" I replied, full of sadness.

"You need to show up at the Board of Director's meeting as planned, except you will be chairman of the company which just bought a large chunk in the resort. You will get the regime change you wanted at the resort, it's up to you who will be the new General Manager." he explained as I listened while in shock.

"Why me?" I asked somberly.

"Because he knew you are capable of much more. According to him you are an intelligent young man who will carry his company on into the future for decades to come. He was giving you a job interview and you didn't even know it." Janowski continued to explain, "He saw leadership capabilities in you and knew that you care about fairness and honesty. You care about the well-being of others and that was a very important quality to Scotty. Congratulations, Mr. Abbott, you are now the Chairman of the Board at his company."

I dropped the phone in the sink and quickly grabbed it. "Is this a joke?" I asked, still in shock.

"No, this is not a joke, Mr. Abbott. Come on up to Scotty's condo and we'll sign the paperwork and make it official. We won't announce the big news until the board meeting. Scotty wanted it to be dramatic. He liked to make an impression in an exciting way."

"I believe that." I said with a smile through my tears.

"I'll see you soon, right?" he asked.

"Yeah, I have to be at work soon." I replied, "I'll be there in about an hour.

"Thank you, Mr. Abbott." he said.

"Thank you, too." I said, and please tell Scotty's wife how sorry I am."

"You can tell her yourself when you get here. I know she will appreciate it." he said.

"Okay, I will. Good-bye Mr. Janowski.

"See you soon."

In a daze of a mixed pot of emotions I placed my cell phone down on the kitchen counter and slowly slid down the side of the wall. I sat in the floor and cried. I pulled myself together; I left my apartment and drove to work.

When I arrived at work, like always, I had to walk past the front desk to get on the elevator. Hilary was waiting to pounce.

"Awwww" she smirked, "does someone have a sad face because they know somebody is getting fired? Poor baby!"

"No," I replied, "I'm sad because Scotty died, I have no sadness about you getting fired."

"What?" she said with a laugh, "Me? Uh, I am not getting fired."

"Whatever makes you feel better." I replied, "If that will help you get through the day, then so be it. Just do me a favor-"

"And what would that be?" she snarled.

"Learn something from this experience so it doesn't happen to you again at your next job." I stated.

"I'm not the one getting a new job." she smirked.

"You're right," I added, "you're probably not, especially after the places that you put in an application with will call here for a reference. After all, this is your most current job and they will call and I will tell them the truth."

"I'm not the one who is losing their job today." she said as if I had lost my mind.

"Another good point," I replied, "tomorrow you will lose your job, not today."

I stepped onto the elevator. When I arrived at Scotty's condo his wife and the lawyer were waiting for me.

"Good afternoon, Mr. Abbott," Mr. Janowski said greeting me at the door, "we have been waiting for you. Come in and let's talk about your future."

CHAPTER 21:

AMELIA GETS BUSTED, I GET FIRED, AND I LIKED IT

It was later on in the evening, and I had just stepped into the elevator when it stopped on the 6th floor. When the door opened Amelia and some gentleman in a swagger suit stepped in. She had a wedding ring on, but he did not. I could have sworn I saw them let go of each other's hands quickly as the door slid open, but I couldn't be for certain that is what I noticed.

"There's some trash on the elevator floor. Someone dropped a napkin or some toilet paper." the gentleman said, stating the obvious.

"Well, I'm not going to pick it up," replied Amelia, "that's what we have employees for; to deal with the unpleasant aspects and anything that might have diseases. I'm too important to worry about what might be on my hands."

"I know what was on your hands a few minutes ago." he whispered loudly into here ear.

"Sshhh! Don't talk." she replied, worried that I might have heard. I did.

"It's kind of ironic," I said, "there are other things than napkins that can carry diseases if you touch them."

They both looked stunned at my comment, not so much

because I had any idea what they were doing a few minutes ago. It could have been completely innocent such as picking up dog poop and changing a diaper, but they knew exactly what they were doing and they gave themselves away by their facial expressions.

"How is that ironic?" the man asked.

"Don't talk to him!" demanded Amelia as she pulled her hair back into a bun. "He doesn't know what he's talking about. He works as a security guard for Christ's sake, he's not smart enough to explain or understand his own comments."

She knew I had a college degree. I just smiled and tried not to laugh at her embarrassment that I caught her with a man other than her husband. I was definitely getting fired now to keep her from worrying if I told anyone.

"Pick that trash up on your way out of the elevator!" said Amelia sternly to me, as they stepped out of the elevator, "and then come to my office in five minutes! I want to speak to you a minute."

Five minutes gave me enough time to go smoke a cigarette and think more about what Scotty's lawyer had discussed with me earlier in the day. I also couldn't help but to think of Sophia, but that's a completely different story for another day.

I walked into Amelia's office. She was sitting there with her arms folded, waiting on me.

I laid the dirty napkin on her desk.

"What are you doing?" yelled Amelia as she swatted the air, "get that nasty thing off my desk! Do you think that's funny? What is wrong with you?"

"I'm just a security guard," I replied, "I'm not able to think things through and know what I'm doing."

"Well, not anymore. I'm letting you go." she said as the corner of her lips curled upwards.

"Why?" I asked, then not really wanting an answer.

"I could give you a dozen reasons, Abbott, but I'm not wasting my breath on you another minute. Get out of my office. Leave your security uniform and badges, cap and anything else in the security office before you leave."

"Actually," I replied, "I feel like I deserve a reason, but I have the feeling it's only because I'm educated, smart and could one day be a risk to your job-"

"You are absolutely no threat to me," she replied, "I just don't like you and neither does Hilary. You don't belong here. This is my resort; do you understand me? People like you don't fit in - and I'll be damned if you think I could ever lose my job to you!"

"I guess with Scotty gone there's nothing stopping you from firing everybody." I said, wanting her to talk.

"Scotty, could have ruined me by not giving us that one-million dollar gift. If he had changed his mind because of me it would have cost me my job. Luckily, the old pompous bastard died and now the resort will get its million-dollar gift, on my watch, and I'll bring this place into the future and no one is going to get in my way. I'll be right here a long time and you will be unemployed." she explained as she finished with a sad face, trying to make fun of my current position.

"It was a pleasure before I had to work for you, and best wishes in the future." I said as I stood up to leave. 'I'm sure you will get everything you deserve."

"I already have." she replied with a grin.

"Just about." I said as I walked away.

I walked out and stopped at the front desk where Hilary was eating a salad. I knew that she was probably given a raw deal in life and that her attitude was a way to put up a wall to protect herself from imaginary scrutiny and biased attitudes, which, in all honesty was probably how she was treated as a child - with name-calling and being made fun of and talked about in whispers right in front of her face. The problem was that now, here, in the adult world it should have been easier on her, but Hilary wouldn't forgive nor forget and carried those feelings with her and displayed them to everyone she knew and worked with. This was a defense that kept her from being hurt by hurting others and throwing the blame and scrutiny on others whom did not deserve it any more than she did as a child. It wasn't her fault she was probably treated horribly by other children, but as an adult the responsibility of her actions and attitude was solely her own doing, and that was not one person's fault but her own.

"Hilary, I want you to know that I am sorry for what ever happened in your life for you to be a bitch to everyone else and treat all who know you poorly unless it can benefit yourself." I said sincerely, "I want you to know that deep inside I know there is a good person in your soul - and for future reference it is better to be nice than to be jealous and hate others, because smiles are contagious, but anger and hate spreads like germs. The only way to stop the resentment is with a kind word, a good deed and a smile. I am very sorry that I treated you the way I did, no matter how much you deserved it. I wish you the best in life and hope that one day soon you are very happy with your life and can smile because it comes natural."

"Uh, I'm not the one who just got fired, so, see ya!" she said with a smirk.

"Just think about it, please." I replied.

I could see in the reflection of the windows as she gazed down at the desk and possibly was thinking about what I had just said, and understood that it was also an apology on my part, for the way

I had acted towards her in return.

Sometimes a little encouragement is all someone needs. Whether they are 14, 32, or 86 a kind word can give someone the energy and ambition to finish what they started, or just start something at all. Only insults and shrugs from ugly mugs can deter our paths, but remember; Encouragement comes from happiness and hope; while insults are just an expression of jealously. Either way, I'm doing something right.

I walked outside into the cold night air and put on my aviator shades. It began to rain. I could feel the tap of rain drops as they hit my sunglasses. With each drop on the lenses I blink. I only wear them to keep the rain out of my eyes. It's a dark moment as I look up at all that falls around me, yet I still stand here amongst the cold, unforgiving rain. I still stand. Soaked now, there is no reason to run for cover. I walk slowly to my car. I am in control. All that falls around me, yet I still stand.

CHAPTER 22:

THE REALIZATION OF HAPPINESS: 'SPORKS', NOT SPOONS

I stopped at the grocery store to buy deodorant and plastic uten-sils on my way home from work. My dishwasher didn't wash the way it was supposed to, and I hated washing everything in the sink, so to avoid a higher water bill I bought plastic cutlery. Why? Because I'm a man. That's how we roll at some point in our lives, usually always before marriage, or after divorce.

The dinky, soft, grocery store music was lightly playing in the speakers. I don't know what it is about the sound of background children-sounding music that makes the power-that-be think that this music is comforting, but it just makes me want to get out of there as soon as possible.

My goal, as stated a moment ago, was to simply buy plastic cut-lery and deodorant, but like almost any plan in life I was now de-toured towards the cookie isle, the pizza isle, and then the cereal aisle, and milk.

Finally, I found my way to the hygiene isle where I found my deodorant. Then I pushed my cart over to the picnic supplies for plastic spoons.

I couldn't find the spoons. There were plenty of brands of forks, knives and sporks, but no spoons. "What the hell? Are you kidding me? Where are the fucking spoons?"

"Can I help you find anything?" a grocery store employee asked me after my explicit thought that came out verbally.

"Yeah, I'm looking for the plastic spoons, but I don't see any." I explained as my eyes continued to search the shelves, hopelessly. "Does nobody ever use plastic forks any longer? Apparently nobody wants the forks now-a-days. It's all about the spoons. Looks like you can't keep them in stock."

"We do have plenty of sporks," he said, as if he was a spork salesman, "they're almost a spoon, yet with that fork end, which might I add, comes in handy when you suddenly need to poke something that cannot be picked up with a spoon."

I looked at him. At the moment I couldn't imagine what I would be eating with a spoon and suddenly feel the urge to need to poke it with a fork. Thank God for a spork or else I would have to get the hell up out of my chair and go get a fork so I could poke my cereal.

In the past I would have imagined myself slapping the shit out of him, but I understood that he was just doing his job and trying to help a customer with their plastic spoon needs.

"Spork?" I replied, "I don't trust hybrids... and besides, a spork is like raising someone else's baby. No matter how much you raise it as your own spoon, you're always going to see that little bit of fork that it's made of. Just sayin'."

"Huh-huh-huh." he laughed.

"Well, sometimes what we want isn't always what we get, so we have to compromise and go with it." I added as I grabbed a box of sporks. "I'll go with the sporks."

"Good choice!" he said with a braces-filled mouth.

I realized that, in a weird way, my trip to the grocery store to buy plastic spoons and ending up with sporks was a metaphor to my life. I didn't get exactly what I was hoping for, but it would work just the same. I accepted it and was content. Strange, but true. I had a moment of clarity and smiled out of the corners of my mouth as I walked up to the cashier.

"Paper or plastic?" she asked.

"It doesn't matter. I'm fine with either." I answered.

She looked at me as if I had a deformed face or some sort of retardation that affected her ability to look at me like a normal person. Then I realized that she had no clue what to put my groceries in, because without an answer she didn't know what to do. I never wanted to be that way in my life. If someone couldn't make a choice... I wanted to be able to make one myself without going blank and not being able to function.

Up until a week ago I wasn't sure how to function in life if I wasn't a journalist, and then suddenly I realized that my paper or plastic was being a journalist or becoming an author. They were both similar and filled people's life with information and entertainment - one was just slightly different from the other.

"I'm going to write a book!' I exclaimed as she flinched at my comment. "I'm going to write a book!"

Paper or plastic, sir?" she asked again.

"Surprise me!" I replied, "I can be happy with either one."

"Okay..." she quietly said as she continued to check-out my groceries and place them in plastic bags.

When I got home I was so very tired that I put the toilet paper in the refrigerator and put the milk on the back of the toilet. I didn't notice until the next morning.

CHAPTER 23:

TIME TO PUT THE SLAP-DOWN ON AMELIA'S BITCH-ASS

I woke up from a weird reoccurring dream that always ended the same way regardless of how it begins...

Standing somewhere on the edge of insanity, across the mountain of obscurity I looked at my hands as they held a red pen and a yellow cigarette. I threw the pen on the dry dusty ground and stepped on it with my left boot sole as I slowly twisted my foot back and forth to put it out. I placed the yellow cigarette behind my right ear to save it for later, for a moment when an idea strikes my soul so that I could write it down on a piece of brown paper wrinkled up in my shirt pocket. I was thirsty, so I walked down a lonely road as I came to a grungy shack with a bright blue neon sign which only read: HERE. I walked inside and sat at a corner table as I swatted at the smoke-filled air. That's when I noticed my old friend, the ogre, across the bar arguing with a couple of sultry women and two weird looking fools. From this point my dreams plays out the same every time: The ogre with the green jelly beans always wins over the bunny rabbit playing cards with the bearded hermit who fight over the rest, only spilling the other colors and left to eat the purple amongst the chaos of overwhelmingly indigenous spirits which come from the ladies behind the bar, across the wrong side of insanity for all to observe and see that their mistake is another one's glory.

Today was the day of The Board of Director's Meeting. I was excited and ready for whatever might happen to happen. I put on my robe and walked the five feet to my bathroom and then took off my robe. I sat down on the toilet for my moment of tranquility.

As I sat on my throne and gazed across my kingdom that morning... well, I couldn't really see much of anything from the toilet, but I could peer across the open bathroom door into my bedroom. That was about it. I could picture it in my head: All I needed was a flat screen TV on the wall in my bathroom, while I sit on my throne and I would be content for about an hour, or so. My legs are numb? Who cares! Gladiator is on! ... "Are you not entertained?!" Yes, I am, thanks.

I reached for my toilet paper as I realized that my half-gallon of milk was sitting on the tank lid. I sighed and just kept sitting there. I picked up a book that I usually read while sitting on my throne. It was a book of inspirational quotes that were there to inspire me while I was doing my 'business'.

I turned to a random page and read a quote by John F. Kennedy.

"When written in Chinese, the word 'crisis' is composed of two characters - one represents danger, and the other represents opportunity."
- John F. Kennedy.

It made perfect sense. It was time to get ready for the meeting. I grabbed the milk and ran to the refrigerator to get the toilet paper.

It was cold. It was very cold toilet paper. That's all I am saying about that.

I was no longer a security officer, thanks to Amelia firing me, so I put on my nicest clothes and left for the meeting.

There was one problem with our grand plan and major announcement. Until it was announced and made official technically, as far as everyone who worked at the resort, thought that Amelia was still the boss and that I was fired, therefore not allowed on the property. I had to figure out a way to get through the gate. It all depended on who was working at the first gate on whether I would get through smoothly, or not.

I thought about just hitting the gas and ramming through the gate. I didn't give a shit; I was in a rental and I had purchased the extra insurance coverage.

When I arrived at the first gate I slowed down to see if I could notice who was working at the gatehouse. I stopped when I saw John walk out to my vehicle.

"Hey, Abbott."

"Hey, John." I replied.

"What are you doing here?" he asked.

"I'm here for the board meeting. I'm meeting with Scotty's lawyer." I said, waiting for him to open the gate.

He laughed a little and shook his head. "No, you're not." he said.

"No, I am. He's already here. Ask him." I explained.

"I mean you're not getting in the gate, Abbott." he replied with a stern voice.

"John, let me explain" I said, "We have a plan all worked out. You just have to wait and find out what it is. Amelia and Hilary are not going to terrorize any one, here, anymore. It's all worked out buddy!"

"Really?" he said as he seemed to be amused, "well, either you're full of shit or crazy, or both, but all I know is you were fired and are banned from the premises."

"John, you're not following me here," I replied, "You don't have to worry, everything is good now. Let me explain. I don't think you understand-"

"Oh, I understand alright!" he interrupted, "I know that you goof-balls and know-it-alls who don't belong here are gone, well, most of you. I know that Amelia is the General Manager and promised to make me the new Head of Security if I gave her all the information on all you disrespectful assholes who were trying to get her fired."

"What?" I mumbled, as I felt betrayed.

"Yeah, she knows everything. I told her everything. That was the deal. I spy for her and she makes me Chief." he said with a grin, "Best of all, she is going to fire Chuck at the meeting. There's going to be a lot of important people there and she's going to humiliate him in front of everyone. I wish I could be there. You on the other hand, if you try to run this gate I'll call the cops and you'll go to jail for trespassing."

"Is that right?" I said as I revved the tiny engine on my electric car rental.

"I would absolutely love for you to run this gate!" he added, "then your ass could get hauled off for destruction of property and trespassing."

"Are you sure about that?" I asked, "Do you promise you will call the police?"

"I dare you." he snarled.

"Okay," I replied, "You got it!"

I sped off but the car wouldn't budge the heavy gate arm. I didn't really do anything except scratch the paint on my little electric car.

I got out of my car and walked into the gatehouse and pushed the button to open the gate. John was on his phone calling the cops when I walked back to my car and drove up the road to the main building at the resort.

I pulled up to the front of the building, leaving my car in the unloading zone. Hilary looked shocked to see me walking through the lobby.

"What are you doing here?" she asked.

I just walked past the front desk and down to the conference room.

When I walked in the meeting had already begun. Mr. Janowski, Scotty's lawyer, was standing next to the door.

"Amelia thinks that I'm here to announce the million-dollar gift." he said quietly, "I didn't lie, or tell her anything, she just assumes that's why I'm here."

"Once she sees me, she's really going to wonder why I am here." I replied.

Within a minute it became quiet. She noticed me standing in the back.

"Excuse me!" she snapped, "Excuse me, what are you doing here!? How did you get in here? Would someone call security please! We have a trespasser here today who is not allowed on resort property!"

I looked around, astonished, pretending to wonder who she was talking about as I finally looked her in the eyes and pointed at myself.

"Call Security, now!" she blurted, "C.F. Abbott you were fired yesterday and are not allowed to be here, especially at this meeting!"

Mr. Janowski took a step forward, "Legally speaking, Mr. Abbott has every right to be here, on the property."

"Especially at this meeting!" I said, eagerly.

"What are you talking about? What's going on here?" she asked.

"I am the legal counsel for S.C. Nerva, LLC." he said, introducing himself. "Mr. Abbott is an employee and Chairman of the company and is here, along with myself, to announce the acquisition of Sugar Peak Resort as part of its holdings."

The crowd began to chatter as a look of confusion spread across Amelia's face.

'That's right!" I said, walking to the front of the meeting where the Board members and Amelia were sitting at a table facing everyone else. "Mr. Janowski is holding the legal documents to show that before his death Scotty set up a new company that bought a controlling stake in this resort. He also made me Chairman of this new company and the President."

"You?" Amelia yelled, as the color of her face drained, "No, no! That's not possible! Upon Scotty's death we were to receive a million-dollar donation to go towards privatizing more of the resort's shares and to upgrade some areas and make extra improvements!"

"I'm sorry, but he changed his mind." Mr. Janowski replied, "he did something much, much better."

"That money was supposed to be mine - to make improvements and, and - and-'

"To make yourself look better?" I added, "Money doesn't make anyone look better. Only a person's soul and the ability to want to do good deeds can make someone look better. And you have neither."

Amelia's jaw dropped.

Mr. Janowski placed his briefcase on the table where the board was sitting. "For anyone interested in reading the documents, I have copies here of Scotty's will and the formation of S.C. Nerva, LLC and the purchase of controlling rights to this resort." he stated.

"Before we do all that legal stuff, I have a recording of Amelia, I think you should all hear." I said as I pulled a voice-recorder from my jacket pocket.

"You are absolutely no threat to me," she replied, "I just don't like you and neither does Hilary. You don't belong here. This is my resort, do you understand me? People like you don't fit in and I'll be damned if you think I could ever lose my job to you! ... "Scotty, could have ruined me by not giving us that one-million dollar gift. If he had changed his mind because of me it would have cost me my job. Luckily, the old pompous bastard died and now the resort will get its million dollar gift, on my watch, and I'll bring this place into the future and no one is going to get in my way. I'll be right here a long time and you will be unemployed."

"Oh, and by the way, Amelia is having sexual relations with that man right there!" I said, pointing to one of the board members sitting at the table next to Amelia.

He looked surprised and Amelia sunk down in her chair with a look of complete shock and shaking her head as if she knew nothing about it. The room filled with gasps and talk.

We waited for the noise to calm down.

Two police officers walked in. Mr. Janowski met them in the middle of the room and showed them the documents.

"Amelia, you just don't fit in here," I said, "I'm sorry, but you're fired."

"Please escort Mrs. Amelia Gant off the premises." Mr. Janowski said to the police officers.

"One more thing," I said as I looked for Chuck in the audience of condo owners and shareholders. "Chuck, you're a good friend. I trust you completely and you are the real management behind the management. I would like you to be the General Manager here. What do you say?"

He smiled and nodded his head. I knew it was more for me and how proud he was at what I had done, but whether he wanted the job or not, he walked up to me and shook my hand.

"Anything for you, Abbott. I mean, Boss." he said with a smile.

"I don't know how you did it, but-" Chuck couldn't finish his sentence; he was so baffled and thrilled.

"It was the right thing to do." I replied. "Hey, I'm not going to tell you how to run this place, you know better than me, but I do want you to fire that Benedict Arnold at the gatehouse."

'Who?"

"John." I said.

"John?" he replied, stunned.

"Trust me." I said.

"I trust you." he replied, "except when it comes to driving anything with wheels."

"Would you believe that I wrecked riding a horse one time?" I asked.

"Yes, yes I do." Chuck chuckled.

"Congratulations Mr. Abbott, and to you too, on your new promotion." Mr. Janowski said to me and Chuck.

"Thank you for all of your help." I said, shaking his hand.

"It was my obligation as Scotty's attorney - and my pleasure." he said.

"Now, time to go fire Hilary!" said Chuck as he smiled, eagerly waiting for that moment.

"I have a better idea." I responded, "You can fire her, but then I want you to hire he back, immediately."

"Why? Are you okay, Abbott?" he said, worried.

"It'll be for a different job, if she wants to take it." I explained.

He looked at me, confused and curious.

"Trust me." I added, "We're better than Amelia. We aren't going to stoop to her level by firing everyone who we don't like, just because we don't like them. It's for the best. Trust me, Chuck."

"I trust you." he replied.

CHAPTER 24:

LIFE'S DETOURS LEAD TO WONDERFUL PLACES

I drove up to the first gate in my newly painted old crappy blue car.

"Can I help you?" Bo said from the gatehouse window. 'I'm just kidding!"

"How are you doing today, Bo?" I asked.

"Great!" he answered, "I got the cast off of my leg yesterday!"

"That's great, buddy!"

"Yeah. So, how's everything with you?" he asked.

"Great!" I replied, "I have a few guests on their way up for the party. Their names are Jake and Sophia. They'll be here in a few minutes, hopefully."

"You got it, Boss!"

"Don't call me, Boss, Bo." I said, "I'm just Abbott."

"Okay," he replied, "watch out, I'm getting ready to raise the gate!"

"Alrighty." I replied as I cringed a little, but everything was fine.

I drove to the top and parked in the owner's lot. Even though I had new paint on my old crappy car it still didn't look like it belonged in the parking lot. I climbed back in and moved to the employee parking area.

As I walked in the service entrance I saw Jerry and Rocky talking.

"Hey, man!" Jerry said.

'How you doing there, young man?" Rocky greeted me.

'I'm great, how are you guys doing?"

"Great." Rocky replied.

"Everything's good as can be." Jerry added.

I noticed Hilary in the lobby pushing her housekeeping cart.

"The condo that your guests are staying in is clean. If they need anything tell them to call the housekeeping office." she said as I passed by.

"Thank you, Hilary, I really appreciate it." I replied.

"Oh no! Everybody pretend like they're working!" Chad exclaimed, "The boss is here!"

"Chad, don't call me the boss. I'm just Abbott, dude." I replied

"Oh, I know that.' he answered with a laugh, "I was talking about Chuck, he just walked in the lobby a few feet behind you!"

I turned to greet Chuck as he walked up to the front desk.

"What's going on, brother?"

"Just the usual." he replied.

We walked into his office and I sat in the same chair that I was first hired in and then fired.

"So, how is the man who made all this possible," he asked with a content smile, "and how's it feel to know you made us all happier and has everything he could ever want?"

I shrugged. I thought about Sophia and couldn't wait to see her again.

"I don't have everything.' I replied, "I never did get to be a journalist." But my thoughts weren't on journalism, as much as they were thinking about Sophia.

Chuck chuckled and shook his head. "How's the book writing

going?" he asked, "Are you getting a lot of writing done?"

"Yeah, actually, I am. It's going well, but I just feel like something's missing." I replied.

"What would that be?" he asked.

"Abbott! Your guests are here." said Chad from around the corner of the door, "Jake and Sophia."

"The girl of my dreams." I answered.

"Well, don't sweat it buddy. I knew Jenn was the one I was going to marry the first time I met her. You'll meet the girl of your dreams one day. She'll show up when you least expect it." he said.

"I'm afraid she already has." I replied.

- But, that's another story, for another day...

THE END.

CPSIA information can be obtained
at www.ICGtesting.com
Printed in the USA
BVHW071341301219
568126BV00022B/1291/P